GHOSTS OF VENTURA

Southern California's Haunted Coastal Community

By Richard Senate

Illustrated by Richard Senate and friends.
Cover design by James C. Cannon

DEL SOL PUBLICATIONS
www.delsolpublications.com

Dedicated to Reverend Edmund Foard
of the Church of the Comforter, Santa Barbara
who helped Debbie and I on our
first steps into the spirit world.
Rev. Foard, I hope you are enjoying Summerland.

I would like to thank the following
people for all of their help in his project:
First, My Wife, Debbie Senate,
My daughters, Sarah and Megan,
My friends John Miller and Katie Crawford.

Fourth **Edition 2004**
Enlarged and expanded.
Original Title: Haunted Ventura

Richard Senate web site:
www.ghost-stalker.com

Del Sol Publications web site:
www.delsolpublications.com

ISBN: 0-9722936-1-2

Book edit and layout by Del Sol Publications.

Table of Contents

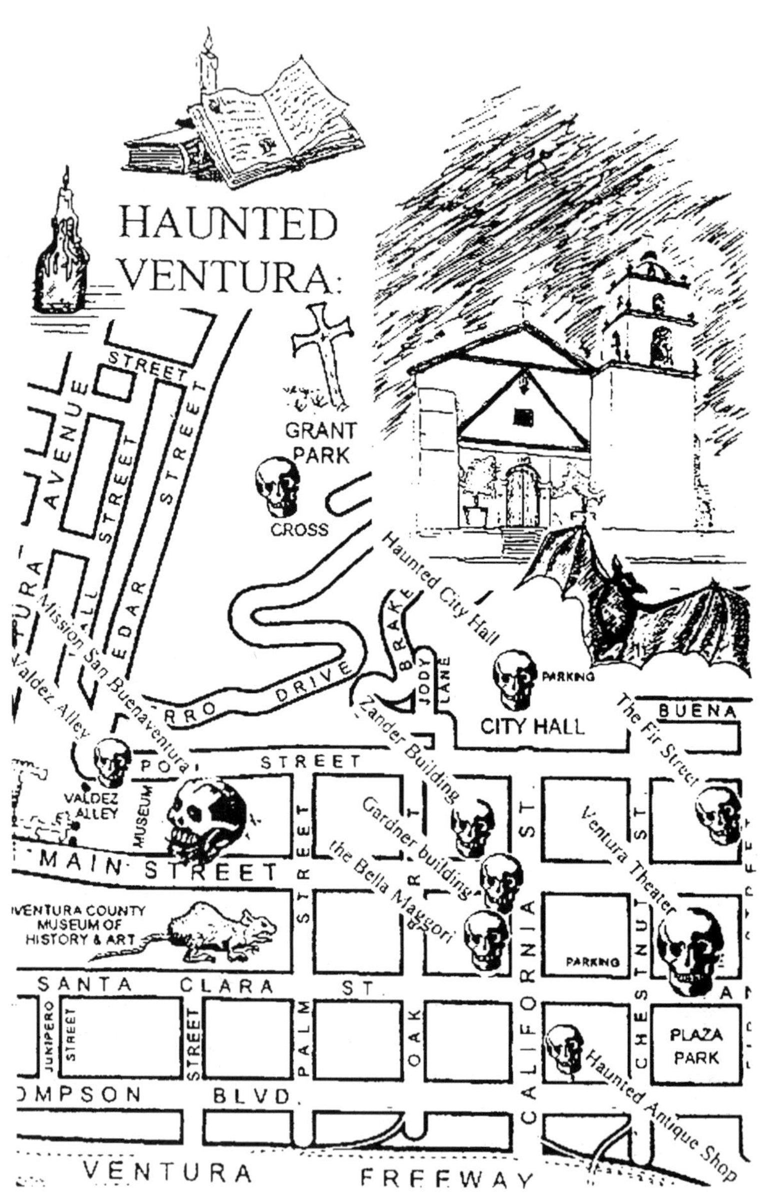
HAUNTED
VENTURA:
GRANT
PARK
CROSS
Haunted City Hall
PARKING
CITY HALL
BUENA
The Fir Street
Mission San Buenaventura
Valdez Alley
VALDEZ
ALLEY
MUSEUM
Zander Building
Gardner building
the Bella Maggori
Ventura Theater
MAIN STREET
VENTURA COUNTY
MUSEUM OF
HISTORY & ART
SANTA CLARA ST.
PARKING
PLAZA
PARK
Haunted Antique Shop
JUNIPERO
STREET
PALM
OAK
CALIFORNIA
CHESTNUT
BLVD.
VENTURA FREEWAY
DRIVE
JODY
LANE
STREET

Introduction

A drive down Ventura, California's Main Street late at night is like a drive back in time.

There is the old Spanish Mission, ancient, forbidding, looming large and stark in the moonlight. It was first established when the boot of Spanish Imperialism dominated half the known world; built to control the native Chumash and make them part of Spain's Empire. Such places all over the globe are haunted.

There are buildings from the Nineteenth Century, reflecting the desires of the Yankee newcomers, with building styles as diverse as Eastlake, Gothic, and Victorian. These were the buildings erected by the greedy, drawn to this land by the lust for gold, and bound here to slake their unquenchable ambition. It is said that such people make the most persistent of ghosts.

There are also the Twentieth Century homes with Spanish tile and sweeping Craftsman's lines; modern homes that face out towards the ever-changing sea; homes built with creative drive by those who place success above all earthly virtues.

Ventura is now famous for it's wonderfully quaint downtown, it's contribution to the sport of surfing, it's Hollywood film connection and it's place in California's rich rancho-era history, but few may know that Ventura is a most haunted place.

Ventura has its own distinct atmosphere, a magic that will always drawn creative and gifted people to her bosom. Such creative individuals see the world in a different way. Yes, such people do become ideal haunting ghosts! If my research is true, Ventura has more than its share of phantom residents. You could even make a case that Ventura, this historic city on the coast, is one of the most haunted places in all California if not the entire west! Look over these accounts I have collected and see if you agree.

The Bella Maggiore Inn
at 67 S. California Street, Downtown Ventura.
The lobby is delightful and the cuisine memorable at
Nona's Courtyard Café & Wine Bar, located at the Inn.

Sylvia, The Ghost of the Bella Maggiore

The elegant Bella Maggiore Inn in downtown Ventura has been restored to resemble an Italian palace. But, behind the serene atmosphere, there may dwell the restless spirit of a suicide or murder victim named "Sylvia."

The historic Bella Maggiore was courageous enough to invite me to lead a team of "ghost hunters" to examine reports of hauntings in an attempt to learn if the stories are true. If the information we gathered is correct, the team discovered the real identity of the sad phantom.

The group consisted of fourteen members that included laymen, psychics and myself. We conducted a number of experiments and spent the night in the beautiful Inn. Promptly at midnight, we ended the evening with a seance. During the twenty-four hour ghost hunt, several strange events were reported.

Mrs. Connie King, of Long Beach, has believed herself psychic for years. Mrs. King was not surprised when she had a number of experiences in the old Inn. *"In my room, I saw the closet door open by itself. Later that night, about 3:47 a.m., I woke up and saw a long white light hovering in the closet door. The room became very cold and I saw a figure at the corner of my bed. It just kept standing there. Finally it vanished."*

Mr. William Johnson, also of Long Beach, was touring the Inn late at night. At approximately 2:00 a.m. he was downstairs in the lobby when he heard footsteps coming down the stairs. They were not steady footfalls but bouncy, *"like someone dancing."* When he looked, there was no one there. He then caught the fragrance of rose perfume. *"I just felt it was a woman. In my mind's eye I could almost see small dainty feet dancing down the stairway."*

During the seance several told of seeing odd lights and feeling an almost electric force drifting through the room. Mrs. Gilmore reported seeing *"a white presence at the end of the room."* Mrs. Amy Hoffman reported a strange chill filling the room during the seance. Another participant told of *"waves of electric shocks"* racing through her body as she heard buzzing in her ears. During the seance four personalities came through Debbie Christenson Senate who was acting as our medium-channel. One spirit called itself "Mark" and said he was a "hippie." He seemed to have died of an overdose of "horse" and "white cross" in the mid 1960's. Another called itself "Elizabeth" and claimed to be the spirit of a little girl murdered long ago. The third did not give a name but laughed and growled in an evil manner. The fourth was the strongest and identified herself as Sylvia Michaels from Atlantic City. She told of being a prostitute in the year 1937. In loneliness and desperation she took her life by hanging herself in a closet of one of the rooms. She seemed sad and not threatening. The spirit seemed glad that the hotel had been renovated and that so many people were visiting the inn. She likes the men most of all.

One experiment we conducted, before the seance that night, was an attempt to draw the ghost. Each member of the team was to meditate and sketch what they believe the ghost might look like. Many paranormal researchers have concluded that the psychic self may reside in that part of the brain where the artistic talent is housed. Most of the drawings were random illustrations. Many of them depicted men in all manner of dress.

Two of the drawings were startlingly similar in style and detail. They depicted a young woman dressed in the fashion of the 1930's. Could this be the face of Sylvia? Information we gathered indicated that there were consistent reports of a female ghost wandering the old hotel, months later a second team was formed to attempt further communications with Sylvia.

The second group would gather on the eve of Halloween. There a medium and I would meet the cast and crew of a local radio station, Q105's "Woody" Show.

They were just as you might imagine, young, irreverent and demographically perfect for their listeners. The show's host, Woody, was in charge of the group. His side-kick and producer, Jewel, acted as a foil to his off-the-wall humor and quick wit. She was no stranger to radio and easily kept up with the fast pace of the show.

When requested to set up a seance at the historic Bella Maggiore Inn, I asked my wife Debbie to act as medium. She had been ill for more than two weeks and rejected an offer a week before when she was asked to hold a seance for KEYT-TV. She must have felt as though she should make an attempt to help and surprisingly agreed. The radio cast would spend the night at the Inn and do their Halloween morning show live from the "haunted hotel" itself. The seance the night before would add some texture to the show and would be recorded so that sound bites could be added in during the live show with interviews of the hotel staff, Debbie and me.

None of them expected what could happen at the seance. Maybe they thought it was all just another silly gag to poke fun at the expense of the medium and the ghost hunter. What they didn't count on was the presence of another party that night, a ghost named Sylvia. What happened next may be open to debate, but for those who witnessed the evenings events, there could be only one explanation. Spirits were present and they made themselves known!

I have attended hundreds of seances over the years, no two are ever alike. Some are emotion-filled cry-fests, others are cold and businesslike. Some seances are short, others can last three hours or longer.

We gathered in a room off the lobby, around a large round

antique table at the lovely old inn. The hotel provided candles that flickered in the dim light. A video tape camera was set up outside the circle and several tape recorders were set into motion. One of the radio station's crew, Robert, monitored the recordings through a headset. We all held hands as the image of the all-protecting white light was invoked to protect the circle and the spirits were invited to come through.

Debbie went into a deep trance-like state. For several long moments she breathed heavily. There was a stillness in the room. Then she began to speak in a voice unlike her own. It was a woman named "Jennifer" who told of being murdered. It was dramatic, but typical of the things that happen at seances. Then, the presence that called itself "Jennifer" was pushed out by a stronger spirit who identified herself at "Sylvia." Sylvia said she was happy in the hotel and had taken a liking to the Desk Manager, Roger. She said that she liked to have fun with him. She also added that the story she had taken her own life in Room 17 was not be true. She may have been murdered and her body placed in such a way that they thought she had taken her life. She seemed to sense the skepticism in the radio people and openly declared she would make herself known to them this night. "I will touch him!" she said in a husky voice. Just then, "Woody" began to rock back and forth in his chair.

Before the others were sure what was happening, the sound technician's headphones were pulled away from his head and the headset fell off onto the floor! Everyone was holding hands including the sound person! This was witnessed by all of the members of the circle. The sound person broke the circle and reached down to retrieve his headset. The circle acts as a protection for the medium and everyone had been instructed not to break the circle. Records in England exist that indicate breaking a circle can cause harm to the medium and, at least in one instance, a medium died when a skeptical reporter broke a circle. Debbie was seized by some force and her head rammed full force into the hard tabletop. She let out a scream! Everyone in the room was shaken for a moment.

We continued the seance for a short time, when a presence called "Mark" spoke in anger and hate. It may have been the unhappy spirit of a young man who died of a drug overdose in the 1960's. Mark's spirit left and a battered and weary Debbie slowly returned, dazed by the events of the seance.

Woody confessed that he had indeed felt something during the seance. It was as if something was sitting on him or "trying to enter his body." The sound man felt the headset pulled from his ears and apologized for breaking the circle. The next day the radio crew talked about the seance and the very strange things that had occurred. Some listeners were supportive and told them there was no reason to fear spirits. Others wrote the whole thing off as a Halloween prank, a shameless attempt to attract listeners. For all those who were present that night, it was real, all too real. The ghostly lady at the Inn continues to play her friendly pranks and make her presence know to visitors from all over the world.

An architectural element from the courtyard fountain at Nona's Courtyard Café at the Bella Maggiore Inn.

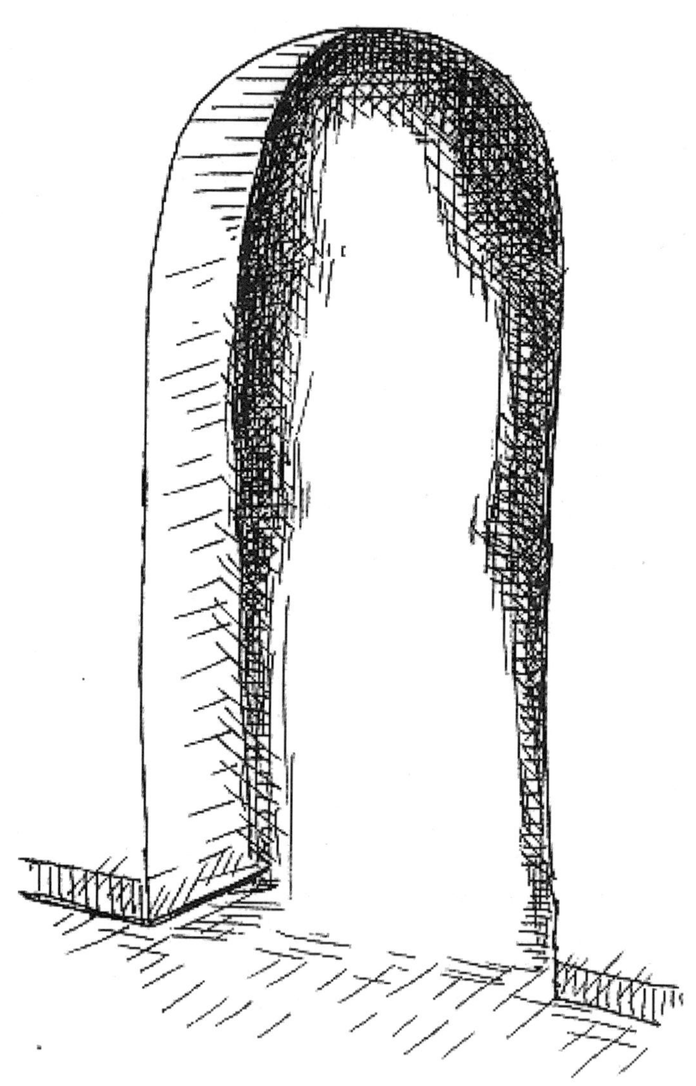

The Fir Street Haunting

It was the first that I had heard that the 1912 home in Downtown Ventura was haunted. The house was part of a program being produced about psychic phenomena called "Borderline." The program later aired on the UPN Network. I was called to investigate the house and determine if it was really haunted. I took a bag full of devises and a local psychic to investigate. I had been told that most of the events happened years ago and I thought that the odds were low that anything would be left to find. I felt the trail was cold and all that we might come up were just a few vague readings and perhaps a stray psychic impression. I was wrong.

The psychic, a very gifted man with a long history of feeling emotional traces and the presence of ghosts, got out of his car and walked up to the house only to feel something push him back! I thought it was just nervousness caused by all of the camera gear and people but, I should have taken it as an omen. We toured the house, without interviewing the people living there. The psychic felt something strike him in the kitchen, the blow almost caused him to reel!

He felt something in one of the door ways and one of the bedrooms in the comfortable and well-furnished home. It certainly didn't look like your traditional 'haunted house'.

I took out the EM meter used commercially to detect dangerous electro-magnetic fields. Ghost hunters have had success using them to locate areas of psychic disturbance and the presence of ghosts. It is thought that the presence of EM fields can indicate places where ghosts are found. Research into this phenomena has been conducted by Duke University.

As soon as I turned it on, the small unit began to read the presence of electro-magnetic fields all over the spectrum! The unit hadn't acted this strangely in all of my investigations. It read dangerous zones only to have them fade away mysteriously. The places the readings appeared, I later learned, were spots in the house where odd footsteps and apparitions had been seen!

The EM detector found that a sort of invisible line ran though the home confirming the places the psychic had felt things. I put the EM unit away and tried a device called a 'Cyber Probe' that measures static electrical fields. A very sensitive device, I had used it in the past to locate places where odd events had been reported. The unit, with its long antenna, began to chirp away immediately! It beeped and sounded when I approached a blue velvet chair. It was going wild picking up a strong static electrical field. It is believed that the movements of spirits cause a detectable alteration in the static electrical field but until now, I had never seen such readings, certainly not with both units in the same place!

The film crew set up their lights and video camera and questioned me about what I had found. I was so amazed at the range of findings I'm not sure how I appeared on camera. They asked "Is this house haunted?" I could only answer "Yes, very haunted." I questioned the intelligent, attractive woman who lives in the house. She told me that the apparition of a woman in a floral print dress had been seen sitting in the blue velvet chair and that the wall, near the doorway, was the place loud knocks and strange footsteps had been heard for years!

There were also the odd fires that had been reported in the house. Three fires with seemingly mysterious origins. The psychic had felt that a little boy had started one of them by playing with matches in the basement. This story was consistent with what the resident said happened many years ago.

The psychic came away with the impression that a woman named 'Mary' once lived in the house and might be one of the ghosts. Records did confirm that a woman by that name had once lived in the home. But the ghost hunt was only half done.

The family who built the house had operated a business in Downtown Ventura only a few blocks from the house.

Today that family's place of business houses the Phantom Bookshop. Long before I had ever heard of the home, I had been told by Mr. John Anthony Miller, the owner of the bookstore, that some ghostly events had taken place in the building. Doors opening and closing, books moving by themselves off the shelves and such things.

I took the two units to the bookshop to see if they would pick up anything out of the ordinary. They reacted with the same dramatic readings! They picked up fields that would suddenly vanish away. It seemed that the same forces that were at work in the house as they were in the bookshop. Both sites exhibited strange events and were found to have confirming EM Fields. It was a most interesting evening and it made an especially interesting segment for the 'Borderline' TV show.

Not All Haunted Houses are Old

The house doesn't look like a haunted house. It's a beautiful split level place with a wide back yard and large picture windows. It looked like the perfect place for Mrs. D to raise her two small children. Then she discovered that the house in midtown Ventura was haunted!

She heard the coughing first. The hack that seemed to echo though the rooms at all hours of the night. Believing that the sounds were from her children, she checked, only to find them peacefully asleep and no one else in the house. She tried to rationalize the odd sounds as the product of the wind or maybe "settling" of the house. That was before she started to feel what she began to call "the presence." It was the unnerving sensation that someone or something was watching her. Many times this feeling would overcome her while she was alone in the bathroom. It was almost as if someone was with her, watching her as she showered. "It gave me the creeps!" she commented as she recalled the haunting presence that seemed to envelope the dwelling.

It was when she was trying to sleep that the ghost was most active. At exactly 10:30 each night she would wake up to feel an icy cold wind sweep over her face. No windows were open and she was unable to find a cause for the chill. The cold wind came every night almost as if to taunt her and deliberately frighten her. Once she stood up in bed in an attempt to confront the presence and vent her anger at the harassment. In the near darkness of her bedroom she saw it! It was milky white, a blur of foggy energy floating near the doorway. She could make out arms of a sort and what might have been a head. Though she felt that the presence was a man there was nothing in the misty apparition to identify it as such. It suddenly vanished away into the darkness.

The woman began to spend her nights in the living room to get away from the thing. For a time this seemed to offer some peace. Strange things started to happen in that room as well. The lights would behave oddly, blinking as if transmitting a code of some sort. Once, a light bulb began shooting sparks!

On one occasion, as the woman went down the hall towards the bathroom, she heard footsteps coming towards her. They were the unmistakable sounds of hard leather shoes or boots on hardwood floors, there was no one there! The footsteps drew closer then past her and on down the hallway.

Her sister came over for a visit when she heard of the events and produced a vial of Holy Water. She thought that the application of this blessed water would free the home of its unearthly resident. Like doing your own plumbing, a do-it-yourself exorcism can be fraught with dangers. The woman sprinkled the Holy Water in those places where the presence had made itself known. The bathroom, the bedroom, the hallway and the living room were "blessed" and the spirit was instructed to depart. This caused things to become worse! That night the sounds of ranting and raving echoed though the house. Banging came from the attic and the family's cats started to scream and hiss. It was as if the thing was angered that someone had tried to force it from "it's house."

Things continued to worsen. When the woman sat on her bed, she frequently could feel the bed lowering with the invisible weight. The coughing worsened. The backyard took on a sinister feel and the garage seemed strangely cold. She did some research and discovered that the builder of the house had passed away in the place. She concluded that the ghost of the builder was lingering behind, still protecting his house from the newcomers who had suddenly taken up residence in the place. She has contacted experts in exorcism with the hope of casting out the unwelcome spirit. So far the rituals seemed to have been effective because the events that so terrorized the family have stopped. It is hoped that the odd spirit has moved on.

The Haunted Tudor Style House

It started to beep, the beeps became faster as the device approached the "haunted room." It didn't look impressive, somewhat like a transistor radio and a TV remote control with a pair of rabbit ear antennas sprouting from the top of it. It is a strange electronic device said to be able to detect the presence of "psychic activity."

I had received a call from a woman in Camarillo who was interested in studying the paranormal. She had purchased the little machine in kit form, and wanted to try it out in a really haunted environment to see if it could pick up any ghostly activity. I had never heard of such a thing outside of fictional ghost finders depicted in such films as Ghostbusters. I asked her to come to a haunted house in Ventura, a place where half-a-dozen witnesses, including myself, had seen and heard what could be described as a ghost. It was my first experience with the machine and I thought this might be a good way to test it's ability to live up to its advertising.

Going through the house it seemed to go off in all the places where sightings had taken place! When I first saw the unit, a CyberProbe, I thought it would only detect fields of static electricity. I mean that it should only beep near curtains and electrical outlets and it did seem to beep near curtains and bed clothing, but it also seemed to go off by itself as if ghosts were moving about in the house. The little beeping unit had passed it's first test. The woman doing the experiment handed me the information she had been sent with the kit. Listed was information of the history of the CyberProbe and how it has been used by the psychic-underground. It seemed to be an extremely sensitive dynamic field detector.

The unit, so it seems, doesn't detect ghosts themselves, rather it detects the electronic impression invisible phantoms leave as they move through the environment. The unit works in "real time." It can't detect where ghosts have been, rather it beeps where they are active!

Even if the simple test was faulty, I must admit I had a great deal of fun trying to trace down the fields of charged energy. But a better test was needed and I sent the woman out to a home on Dunning Street in Ventura, where several ghost sightings had been reported by a terrified family.

The team went in alone, for I didn't want to influence them one way of another. Once again the little probe managed to focus on the stairway where some of the most dramatic events had been felt. The group even felt a distinct chill when they seemingly passed through a ghost! The residents confirmed that they too had the same thing happen to them. The second test indicated that the CyberProbe might be an interesting tool for investigations.

The Doctor Returns

In the course of psychic investigation it is really rare that a case comes along that has the elements of what is called a "best case." By that it is meant that the case seems to offer evidence of an existence beyond the grave. Such a case was reported to me recently.

The doctor was well-known and well loved. His patients sought him out, so well were his skills known in the community. He was a happy man with many friends and a promising future. But, a sudden illness befell this man and his time on earth was trimmed short.

Everyone who knew him was saddened by his untimely end. In his office, the office manager was perhaps the most stricken. She could not bring herself to attend the funeral and only attended the grave site services. She never saw the casket open; she didn't think she could bear to see her friend resting in a casket.

She continued to work at the office as other staff members found other places to work. Working late one night, she turned to look up from her desk to see the doctor with his grey hair and wearing a distinct grey pinstriped suit. The image didn't look at her, but as he moved down the hallway he turned his head from right to left as if he were seeing things. She vowed to stop working so many overtime hours.

A new nurse was hired who had not known the deceased doctor. Several weeks later the new nurse was in the office late one night by herself and looked up to see, in the same hallway, a man with grey hair and a grey pinstriped suit.

She had never seen the deceased and she had not heard of the first encounter but she described seeing the same man doing the same thing, looking in several directions. When the office manager heard of this, her heart skipped a beat. Later, it came to her that the grey suit the apparition wore might be significant and called a friend who had attended the funeral service with the open casket. She learned that the doctor had indeed been buried in a grey pinstriped suit!

What makes this a "best case" is that there were two sightings of the same phantom. Each sighting was independent, and each sighting described the same actions and location. One of the sightings was from a witness who had never seen the doctor. Both sightings were clear about the type of suit the figure was wearing, which turned out to be the kind of suit the man had been wearing when he was buried. It seems that whatever the reason, the spirit, essence, or ghost returned to his office, perhaps to finish some important project. He was looking for something. He didn't seem to be interested in the people who saw him, he didn't even look in their direction. He was on some mission. Whatever it was, it gives some proof that life isn't over at the point of what we call death.

The return of the doctor is only one of a number of cases that suggest that life continues on. Some believe the ghosts that are seen are simply the spirits of the dead returning to accomplish some overlooked deed before they can go on to whatever reward awaits us all.

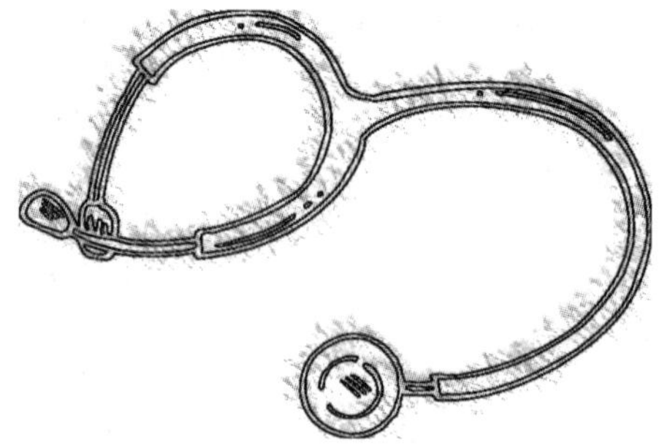

The Haunting of Mission San Buenaventura

The old Spanish Mission San Buenaventura stands stark and white in the sun as it has since its completion in 1809. Its thick walls seem to radiate a supernatural glow even in the brightest noonday sun. But the best way to capture the eeriness of the old church is to pass beside its walls at midnight. Like many of the Spanish Missions of California, it is believed to be haunted! Some of the tales associated with the venerable church may be based upon real encounters with ghosts and spirits. Others may be simply creations of long dead story tellers, told to send chills up the spines of young listeners. As the Spanish say, "Quien Sabe?" Who knows?

The Chumash natives, who lived in Ventura before the coming of the Spanish, believed in the existence of ghosts. They fished the seas in well-made plank boats. They were brave and skilled seamen. Their courage was proven by the fact that they believed that those who drowned at sea would come back as wandering ghosts. They would never be able to enter the heavenly abode. Perhaps that is why the phantom Native American maiden wanders the mission. The woman wears a long white dress stained with sea water. Her long black tresses are soaked and her face is deathly white with oversized eyes.

Those eyes can send an icy chill into those unfortunate enough to encounter this troubled spirit. One witness told of smelling the pungent odor of rotting seaweed just before he turned and saw the pale apparition. Sometimes just her eyes are seen floating in the air.

Late one night a man was returning to his car parked near the old mission. He felt strange, as if someone was watching him. When he got to his car, the man quickly turned around and saw two glowing eyes about ten feet from him. He watched speechless as the glowing eyes floated back, retreating toward the mission church. The sad ghost is not a malevolent spirit, perhaps only desiring prayers or recognition to assist it on its heavenly path.

Others tell amazing stories of the thick walls of the mission church. The six and a half foot thick walls of stone and adobe are believed by some to contain bodies. Indians and padres are said to have been interred in those walls centuries ago. Records kept by the missionaries clearly show that the walls were never used to inter the dead.

Remains of three early padres at the mission are indeed buried beneath the alter of the church. Behind the mission, a monument to these pioneer priests has been built. Perhaps the monument has inspired the stories of bodies in the walls. Checking the early record, one finds that four not three padres were buried under the altar. The identity of the fourth priest is unknown, if he ever existed. Perhaps he is the ghostly monk reported at the mission for the last hundred years?

The image in a gray robe has been reported in the courtyard of the mission. Also he is seen along certain downtown alleys and once at the mouth of the Ventura River, near Hobo Jungle. One thing is certain, in the early years, the apparition was never seen inside the church. This has led to speculation that the ghost monk is somehow unable to enter the church building, but recent encounters have taken place within the church itself. Some believe he is cursed to walk the mission. We can only guess what terrible sin this unfortunate committed to be given such a sad penance. The gray-robed figure is not a terrifying specter. One witness even reported that the image was wearing a large smile as it vanished before her eyes

Recently several young girls, parishioners at the mission, claim to have seen a woman gliding down the center of the church while clutching a glowing rosary. At first the girls thought that she was just another worshiper until they noticed that she was floating about half a foot above the floor. Thcy ran from the church and were convinced that she was a religious ghost.

By far the most frightening tale linked to the mission may be only a story. It is said that on certain nights of the year, a headless horseman rides down Ventura Avenue and then down Main Street. The hideous apparition is said to be the unclean soul of a terrible desperado of the last century. A man so evil, he sold his soul to Satan. This outlaw was hunted down near Ojai and killed by lawmen over a hundred years ago. Thinking he might collect a reward, a member of the posse severed the head from the corpse before its burial in a hasty grave. Because of this sacrilegious act, the ghost rides forth from the pit of hell, seeking vengeance on those that desecrated his body. They say the hoof-beats of his hellish stallion are heard just before midnight. Then the black-garbed figure rides into view. The huge mount, a demonic black stallion, snorts flames, sulphur and brimstone from its enlarged nostrils. The outlaw, having no head or eyes, takes vengeance on any whom he contacts. He uses his glowing lasso to capture his victims and jerks the souls from their bodies. He then takes their souls back to his abode in the netherworld of Hades. If by chance you hear the ominous hoof-beats, they say you have only one chance to escape the headless horseman. Run as fast as you can to the steps of the Old Mission San Buenaventura. The hellish horseman, being a thing of pure evil, is unable to approach hallowed ground. At the old mission you will be safe.

Mission San Buenaventura,
211 East Main St., Downtown Ventura
The mission is located near an art and history museum, galleries, interesting shops and restaurants, and all steps from the Pacific Ocean. A California experience, a real must!

Night Walkers

The complex of apartments is not quite twenty-five years old, but something old and still active haunts one corner of the structure, something mysterious, something ghost-like.

Some places seem to be charged with a supernatural essence, almost like they attract ghosts and mysterious happenings. The apartment complex in Ventura seems to one of those places.

In one apartment, the resident was about to retire for the night when she saw a form walking down the hallway. It was late, between one and two in the morning. She assumed it was only her roommate coming to use the bathroom. But, as it drew near and passed her, she saw that it was the image of a strange man with dark, slicked-back hair. The man didn't seem to look at her, holding a blank look on his face. The overweight man with deep-set eyes just vanished into the darkness. The image didn't frighten her when she saw him. Later, as she was looking at family photograph albums, she saw a long deceased uncle who resembled the image she saw.

Another apartment resident was in the carport of the complex when she saw a ball of fire fly out of one of the windows and swoop over the building.

The event that started the tenants talking to one another was when footsteps were heard on the roof one night. They were heard by a half dozen people. The slow measured footfalls would cross the roof and, when they checked, there was no one there. After that the footsteps were heard more often.

Two men sharing an apartment noticed their cat would avoid one room and would hiss at an unseen presence in that room. A computer in the room was disabled when the keyboard cable was crudely broke by an unknown force. One of the men heard his name spoken and recognized the voice as a deceased relative. Once he saw the face of a woman appear at the doorway of his room, look around the doorsill and vanish.

Upon other occasions he has seen a female form fly over his bed late at night. He too had heard the late night walkers on the roof.

One resident felt her cat jump onto her bed and walk toward her, only to find nothing there. Others tell of feelings as if they're being watched and hearing things. Some report hearing sounds, showers running, voices and footsteps coming from rooms that are vacant. One apartment had lights being turned on and off without any cause.

The apartment is built over an old cemetery and this may be the cause of the supernatural happenings. Research indicates that the building is built on what was a sacred walkway, used on holy days such as the longest and shortest days of the year. Processions of Chumash carrying painted plaques and banners, chanting and playing flutes walked from the beach to the high mountains to address their gods. Perhaps the thousands of years that this was done has charged the area with a psychic power. Maybe the "vibrations" attract ghosts or even people with psychic ability.

There is a theory that states that there are lines of psychic energy. These lines are a network that enmeshes the world. These lines of power converge at points forming crossroads of increased psychic power. The theory holds that these lines of power are naturally felt by man and are selected as sites for temples and church procession routes. It could be that this apartment is built on one of these psychic crossroads. As such, anyone living in one of these places would experience an increased psychic ability that would include seeing deceased relatives, sounds from the past and knowing the future.

Perhaps the walkers are those long dead Chumash tribesmen still walking the sacred procession route. One thing is sure, the residents who live in the haunted apartments get far more than what their rental papers mention.

Ghostly Star

First of all I want to inform those who read this story that I can not tell you where this apartment is located except that it is in a fashionable neighborhood in an older section of Ventura. It is a studio apartment with bright walls and wide windows. The sun shines in the place but it isn't warm or friendly.

A young woman was murdered here nearly three decades ago. She was 19 years of age, attending college with a desire to become a writer of children's books. Her death was as brutal as it was unexpected. The police wrote the crime off to a robbery for drugs and no suspects were questioned and the killer never apprehended.

The young woman who moved into the apartment didn't know the grim history of the place. She saw only the quaint, quiet location, the perfect apartment with ideal rent. She wasn't in the place long before something woke her out of a sound sleep, hands slowly moved around her neck! Even in the near darkness she could see that there wasn't anyone there! Then the unseen hands began to choke her. She managed to fight off the terrible sensation and sit up in bed gagging. She felt scared for her life but, with her bank account what it was after the move, the new tenant was unable to move again. She tried to tell herself that it was all some sort of dream and the odd feeling just a touch of the flu. She didn't sleep the rest of the night and had a miserable day at work. She took some sleeping pills the next night but she felt ill at ease in the apartment as if she were being watched by unseen eyes. She went to sleep but her dreams were filled with images of a young woman with long hair dressed in the style of the 1970's.

It was a neighbor living on the same street who told her of the murder and the name of the unfortunate girl. She spent an afternoon in the library and found the newspaper accounts of the crime and the burial of the victim. When she saw the picture of the young woman in the newspaper, it appeared to be a high school graduation photograph. It was just like the image in her dream! She also discovered that her death had taken place at midnight. The same time she had felt the cold hands around her neck! It was as if she were trying to communicate with the new tenant.

It was about this time that the tenant began to write a children's book. It was as if she was inspired to compose the story of a little girl with her own star that followed her around. The feelings grew stronger in the room and at last the woman was so bothered that she began to talk to the unseen phantom.

At last she felt compelled to call the victim's mother who lived not far away. She was surprised to find out that before her death, the victim had began to write a children's book! It was as if she were somehow influencing her to do the project she had left undone. When the woman finished the book, she visited the grave site of the murdered girl and was shocked to see on the tombstone an engraving of a little angel with a star over her head, like the story she had written!

The presence seemed to overpower the woman and within her a feeling began to grow that the person or persons responsible for the original murder were not far away and wanted to kill her. The stress of the haunted apartment grew too great and the woman at last moved out. The ghost didn't follow and, maybe it still haunts the studio apartment. Maybe she wants to tell her story and indicate who terminated her earthly existence before she can move on to the next world.

So if you have just moved into a nice neat studio apartment where the chill of the night is present even in the afternoons. A place that is wonderful and quiet. A place where shadows drift across the walls and a low sobbing echoes at midnight. In such a place you might dream of a beautiful woman with long hair and a simple smile. You may even be compelled to write a book, maybe a mystery about murder.

Ghost of the Zander Building

If the stories are true, the phantom form of an elderly man in gray wanders the length of the Zander Building on the 400 block of Ventura's Main Street. Today, the building is a collection of small shops and offices, and several shopkeepers report the misty figure strolling the structure. Mrs. Eddie Gullon of Eddie's Treasures, an exclusive metaphysical bookstore, has experienced the phantom. She has operated the bookstore in the historic building since 1987. When she opens her shop early in the morning, she has heard shuffling footsteps following her down the corridor from the parking lot. "It's like someone is walking behind me," Mrs. Gullon explains. "My hair just stands on the back of my neck… it's gotten so bad that I won't come down here early in the morning." Eddie's bookstore is equipped with an electric eye at the doorway to alert her when customers drop in to browse. Often she is in the back room, unable to see who enters. She will hear the bell of the electric eye and then enter the shop to discover no one there. Believing it was prankster, or a malfunction of the electric eye, she has watched carefully, only to discover that the bell goes off by itself from time to time. Could it be, she speculates that the gray ghost is simply stopping by to window-shop?

"If it's him, I hope he buys something" she adds with a smile. Perhaps the spirit is drawn to the establishment because she caters to the metaphysical. Maybe he is reading up on what to do once one is a ghost.

To keep her company, Edie has brought her dog down to the shop several times. "When I take her in from the parking lot, sometimes she just stands there shaking and won't come down those steps" she says. "I have gotten some strange feelings on those stairs myself. It's happened four or five times now. I think she can sense when the ghost is around. Edie has also reported that her shop has become strangely cold from time to time. "It's like a moving cold spot," she describes it. "It seems to be checking up on things." Edie has never seen anything that could be called a phantom, but another shopkeeper has.

Helen Lynch has operated the Cats Meow shop in the Zander Building for the last six years. She has seen the ghost at least three times. *"The first time it was out of the corner of my eye,"* she admits. *"He is a tall man, kind of bent over and*

The Zander Building is a lovely melange of unique shopping. Located on Main Street in Downtown Ventura.

graying in the temples, lanky you would say. He is wearing a loose gray suit. It drapes over his body and I remember the coat was unbuttoned. The suit seemed like it was made out of a linen material. He didn't wear a tie. He looked maybe sixty years old. The first time I saw him clearly, I was talking with my daughter. (I) looked back toward the store room, and saw him come out from the back. He just walked toward us as we sat there talking. I looked at him, looked down, looked up again and he was still there, then he just disappeared. My daughter didn't see a thing, but she was facing the other direction. A short while later I saw him again. This time he was coming out of a doorway. He turned, walked away from me and vanished. It was odd, it didn't scare me at all. I just had the feeling that I didn't want to have any thing to do with it. You would think that seeing something like this would scare the heck out of you; this one didn't."

Hearing the stories of the ghostly gray man, I visited the Zander Building with a psychic to learn if someone else would have the same reactions as the other witnesses.

On a cold, windy day we visited the site. Near the stairway at the rear of the building that leads to the parking lot, the psychic began to shiver all over. "He is here," she murmured. "It's a male presence. He is confused, I feel he is out of place here." The narrow stairs became colder as she spoke. The icy feeling passed and the temperature warmed somewhat. We began to walk the hallway building. She stopped midway. "He moves around; he has so many questions." She held out her hand as the coldness returned. "He is attached to this place and watches over it." The coldness vanished as abruptly as it arrived.

Is the Zander building really haunted? No one can be sure, but the reports persist that a wandering phantom is encountered in its marbled hall.

Ventura Theater
An excellent venue for a concert, or a haunting, located at 26 South Chestnut. Downtown Ventura

Mystery of the Ventura Theater

She danced upon the stage that night, turning and spinning in her own radiance. Theater employee Davy saw the figure for several moments before it abruptly vanished.

"It was about four a.m.," he recalls. *"The stage and everything was all black. Then there was this bright light on stage. It held your eye and I stopped to look at it for about thirty seconds. It was moving around... it didn't scare me but, I couldn't speak. Then it stopped and was facing me, it took a step forward and disappeared. I went up the stairs yelling, "I saw a spook, I saw a spook."* The two-year employee recalls that the apparition looked *"like a white graduation gown!"* Though the image was missing its head, he felt that the *"spook"* was that of a woman.

The old Ventura Theater has long been rumored to be haunted. This was the first time that the ghostly residents put on a show for the crew that maintain the historic theater. Formerly the tales of shadowy figures and phantom voices have dominated the supernatural history of the place. Now the specters are making their way on to the stage. A mystery surrounds the sighting. Who is the ghostly figure and why does she cavort upon the boards?

Inquiring the other members of the staff, several rumors have circulated in an attempt to explain the sighting. One theory holds that, years ago, a graduation was held in the old theater. During the ceremonies one of the students fell to her death from a high walkway behind the stage. This tale fails to confirm when such a tragedy occurred. They cannot even isolate the decade of this accident. If it were true, this would be a classic case of a haunting. If so, the accident must have damaged the victim's head, hence the headless image.

Besides the glowing figure on the stage, other phenomena have been reported. The present stage manager heard a loud piercing scream echo through the hall one late evening. He was at a loss to explain the sound. Perhaps it was the last dying cry of the woman who fell to her death. Another tale attached to the place centers upon a suicide alleged to have happened at the theater years ago. Someone is said to have hung themself in the rear part of the stage. No one could give any facts on the alleged hanging at the Ventura Theater. Why did he or she take their own life? When did such a thing happen? Stories of this type abound in old theaters. I have come across several similar tales found in numerous playhouses all over the world. Theaters have a magic all their own.

The old Ventura Theater has been converted into a concert hall for top Rock & Roll acts and head-liner comedians. This has breathed new life into the aging structure. Built originally to offer legitimate Vaudeville and first-run films, the Ventura Theater is equipped with a large fly gallery, dressing rooms and footlights. Perhaps all the new activity has stimulated old half-forgotten memories that were dormant within the building's walls. Perhaps the memories have taken definite form and now walk the backstage and halls.

The Haunted Antique Shop

On April 18, 1996, I received the following letter. Names have been omitted to protect the owner of the haunted shop that is located in Ventura's historic downtown.

"Let me state at this time in my letter that I'm not one to be considered 'flighty', 'space-y' or 'subject to hallucinations' but I would like to relate a recent experience I've had.

Last December I rented a tiny store so I could open an antique store near downtown Ventura. Given the fact that my tiny store has no bathroom facilities, I was given permission (as well as a key) to use the vacant shop next door to me to take care of my needs. As I was moving my merchandise into my tiny store, a curious neighbor proceeded to tell me about the 'Horrific Fire' that had engulfed my building and the fact that one baby died. Anyway, I never gave it a thought since the building has been nicely renovated for an old relic. Anyway, as I proceeded to unpack merchandise in the vacant store door, since my tiny shop was overcrowded, I had the most frightening experience of my life. (I'm 44 years old and I have been around some I might add.) As I reached down inside a box I felt a firm nudge against my right hip--as if someone was trying to push me. My first thought was of a rapist, burglar, or 'mugger'. For a split second I thought I was going to be a victim of some violent crime. I whirled around, frightened to death of a potential rapist, only to find no one there. I cannot tell you the relief I felt when I realized no one was going to 'get me'. Then, all of a sudden I realized someone did nudge me-gave me a good, hard push. I might mention that there was no way someone could have entered the vacant store where I was unpacking. Since I was actually standing in the doorway of the front door, the only exit in and out of the building, there are no windows that open and the back door is permanently bolted shut.I was facing out towards the street, so no one could have nudged me or touched me without being seen by me first. It is impossible. That was why I was so shocked to feel the push on my hip--no one could have done that under those circumstances. I realized for the first time in my life that ghosts really do exist!

Then a couple of weeks ago, as I was packing everything up to move my tiny business to Ojai, my fiancee told me about an incident he had in the vacant store next door. He was taking a nap on a camper's mat at the back of the shop and heard footsteps, waking him up. He called out my name but when I didn't answer he got up and went to the front. Then he realized that he was all alone. He then went to the back and proceeded to resume his nap. Then he heard tapping on the walls. He fell asleep once more. When he awoke, his blanket was folded next to him, on the floor. There was no way he could have thrown off the blanket much less folded it. He asked me if I took off his blanket and when I said no he said the building must be haunted by a ghost as he explained the phantom footsteps, tapping on the walls, and blanket incident. It was then that I confided in him about my incident of being 'pushed.'

My shop is now out-of-business as of last week, but I'm using it for temporary storage since the rent is so cheap. A few days ago I had a nosy neighbor ask me why I was going out of business. I just told her that I needed a bigger shop. I was too proud to tell her that business was lousy. Anyway, she told me she was surprised I stayed as long as I did (a little over three months). I asked her why she was surprised and she then told me that 'everyone' in Ventura knows this building is haunted and that's why no one wanted to rent my tiny store, or the one next to it. She went on to say that no one will ever go into these stores for any reason, because of the rumors of the hauntings. I told her I didn't know what she was talking about. I was not about to tell her of my experiences since I don't want anyone to think I'm a 'crackpot.' I've done what little research I could on this building and it's true that since the fire about a year ago, the two stores have been vacant despite the fact that they have been nicely renovated and the rent is very cheap. It seems no one wants anything to do with this haunted building. The owner told me they were having trouble renting the place."

The neighbor who stated that people avoided the store because it was haunted was wrong: I have found that haunted places are fascinating to the general public and this seems to lead to increased business. As for everyone knowing that this building was haunted, this is the first I have heard of this and I make it my business to know each and every place rumored place to have ghosts in Ventura. Perhaps, with some research and perhaps investigation, the identity of the phantom and the reason for the haunting will be disclosed.

"I went on Mr. Senate's tour of the City Hall building and when I walked into the old jail on the third floor my hair just stood on end. I saw a figure move in front of the window. It was like a shadow.....and there was no one over there.

I haven't seen ghosts before but I am convinced this was one."

- Visitor from Oceanside

San Buenaventura City Hall, the old courthouse, is the centerpiece of the downtown. The steps provide a great view of Historic California Street. Grand architecture, impressive interiors and an art collection worth seeing at City Hall, 501 Poli Street, Downtown Ventura. City Information 805 654-7850

Ventura's Haunted City Hall

The beautiful Ventura City Hall stands majestically atop Historic California Street in Ventura, like an alabaster temple dominating the skyline. It stands out because it was meant to, designed as the Ventura County Courthouse in 1912. At the cost of $250,000, it is one of the most beautiful civic structures in the state. Few realize that this impressive building is also haunted.

The reports of city hall ghosts have made their way into local newspapers that inspired a local group of actors to produce a multi-part play parodying local politics. This production featured an always fainting ghost hunter they called "Richard Seen-it." Flattery, I guess, can be found in such work. Fortunately, I have a good sense of humor and could only laugh when my bungling name sake fainted when he at last encountered the ghost of Father Junipero Serra.

The ghosts that wander the halls are well known to the police department. Behind the desk of the councilmen, there is a telephone with a direct line to the police department. I guess it is used when a meeting becomes too outspoken. Then the SWAT team can be called out to suppress would be poets and protesters or such. The line, fortunately, has yet to be needed. But long after the building is closed for the night, long after the posturing and debate has ended, the phone has been activated. The police call but there is no one there. Who is making these phantom phone calls and why?

The room has good reason to be haunted because the ornate chamber was used as the Superior Court Room for the County of Ventura for sixty years. It was in this room that a number of very important trials were held. Perhaps the best known was the trial of Elizabeth "Ma" Duncan in 1958. It was one of the most sensational of its day. Reporters from all over the nation converged on Ventura to witness this shocking trial. In many ways "Ma" Duncan was the real mother-in-law from hell. She disliked her daughter-in-law so much that she hired two men to murder her for the bargain basement price of six thousand dollars. But they never received more than three hundred dollars. The old saying that you get what you pay for might apply here. The two ex-convicts proved to be unable to perform the murder without leaving bundles of clues for the police. They even used a car with engine trouble that forced them to bury the body of their victim in a shallow grave near Casitas Springs. The two murderers were soon apprehended and, with little encouragement, pointed the finger at "Ma" Duncan.

Mrs. Duncan proved to have a lurid past and an arrogance that alienated the jury. She denied everything, but her sinister nature won her only contempt. She and her two associates were sentenced to die in the gas chamber. She was the last woman in California to suffer this extreme penalty. The ghost that now wanders the council chambers may be the spirit of "Ma" Duncan. Perhaps she is now remorseful over ending the life of her daughter-in-law and grandchild. The victim was seven months pregnant at the time of her barbarous murder.

If it is "Ma" Duncan who haunts City Hall, she isn't alone. The west wing of the City Hall once housed the County Sheriff's Office and served as County Jail. In its half century of use, it housed numerous infamous criminals including such notables as Charles Manson, Paul Skyhorse and Richard Mohawk. The men's jail has been demolished but the women's jail still exists on the unused third floor, just above the offices of the Parks and Recreation Department. Rumor holds that one of the first women incarcerated in the jail in the early 1940 hanged herself in one of the cells. This nameless woman became the restless spirit that is responsible for mysterious happenings that have occurred. The building was completely renovated before the city took it over for office space in 1971. Even after these changes, the ghosts remain.

One well-placed source tells me that the elevator in this building has a mind of its own. The controls send it from the first floor to second, but to go to the deserted women's jail area a special keys needed. One woman who holds a position in the city government has confided in me. Whenever she takes the elevator, it takes her to the jail on the third floor....she does not have the special key. Touring the dark empty space one can easily imagine how rumors like this might be started. It is a cold and chilling place, a place of intense sadness and despair. Perhaps it is a good thing that this floor wasn't converted into office space.

There is the story of the lady in blue. A psychic woman, a long time Ventura resident, was visiting the second floor of City Hall in 1990. She heard the distinct sounds of high heeled shoes behind her. She turned as the echoing taps became louder and louder. She saw a young woman, dark hair, gleaming red lipstick and wearing a tight blue dress coming toward her. The hair style was that of the mid 1940's, as was the cut of the dress. To her surprise the woman passed her and then vanished with a sudden burst of cold air. Who is this ghostly woman? She seemed to be in a rush to go someplace, walking toward the former Sheriff's offices. The witness claimed that the dress shimmered as if it were made of an expensive material. She doubts that it was a lowly paid secretary or clerk. Perhaps it was the wife of a prominent man in government and she often visited him?

The historic City Hall is a unique place, and an ideal spot to visit. Within the lobby is the city information office where one can find a self-guiding brochure of the building. Unfortunately the third floor is closed to viewing. Maybe someday it too will be featured.

Mr. Senate, I am a native Californian who grew up in Ventura. I have had several, unexplained "happenings" around the Creek Road area and the Ventura County Court House. My sister has joined you on one of your tours. She is very sensitive and open to the paranormal. She has seen the Lady in Blue at the court house. (Evidently the Lady in Blue has developed a liking for my sister) She has visited my sister in her home. My sister understands there is a problem with the elevator this lady wishes to use to go "up". My sister has tried to explain to her she is using the wrong elevator, and the one she wants is broken and she must use another. The Lady stands with her hands held out as if she is asking for help. I am very interested in this line of study. I am not as sensitive as my sister, or maybe I have just not known how to develop my sensitivity. I would like to ask what you know about this Lady in Blue. Why is she seeking something from my sister, and is there anyway to help her cross over and go home?

The Lady of Valdez Alley

"I think I saw a ghost," the woman said, trembling in the warm afternoon sun. "I was looking toward the alleyway when I noticed something moving. It was a woman with long flowing hair and a white dress. I didn't see any feet. It just moved away from me up the alley and just disappeared." The sun was shining on a clear afternoon, yet the woman claimed to have encountered a phantom form.

The narrow Valdez Alley, located just west of the old Spanish Mission in Ventura has been a walkway since the days of the padres. The name comes from the adobe of Ramon Valdez that once stood at the entrance of the alley. Perhaps as early as the Valdez ownership, the alleyway has been rumored to be haunted. Over the decades, numerous individuals have reported seeing a woman in a long flowing dress walking there at odd times.

Some believe the lady in white is the restless spirit of a Chumash native girl who died by drowning while swimming in a rain swollen river. The Chumash believe that drowning is the worst of all ways to die. Such a death insured that the unhappy soul would wander the earth forever unable to go on to whatever rewards awaited in the land of the dead.

One resident of many years tells of an encounter with the white lady almost forty years ago. He described the image as *"the most beautiful woman I had ever seen... all in white. So thin you could see right through it, in the moon light. It was maybe one o'clock when I was coming home.... She just stood there looking down at me from the stairs until she was just nothing. You want to bet I was scared! I went to mass that Sunday, the first time in years."*

Others have seen the mysterious figure in the alleyway. Some describe it as a gray form, a misty figure that slowly drifts up the alley toward the stairs. Several individuals who claim to have psychic ability have walked the alleyway attempting to receive impressions of the lady in white. One woman felt such a feeling of dread that she began to shake all over and could not proceed up the alley. Another psychic saw a figure standing by one of the lampposts. Recently another psychic walked the alleyway attempting to use her gifts to discover the identity of the specter. *"I can feel her now,"* she said with a whisper. *"She is standing nearby. I can see her in my mind's eye. She is wearing a long dress with long sleeves. She is an Indian girl of the mission. She has such long black hair, it's very beautiful. There is something terribly wrong with her. I am getting a name... Maria? Yes, Maria, her name is Maria. There was something wrong with her eyes. They are dark, dark holes in her head. O'God they blinded her!"* Trembling in fear she said, *"They used long wooden pegs to blind her so she couldn't identify the Spanish soldier who raped her."* The psychic walked on ahead toward the stairs, and knelt down on the first step. *"She was attacked here, there were four of them. They used a leather thong in her mouth to keep her from crying out. The poor girl, oh, the poor girl. She tried to go home but she couldn't see. She is still trying to find her way home after all of these years."*

The psychic tried to communicate with the sad spirit to assure her that she could go on to the next world. As the psychic closed her eyes and muttered comforting words, a cool breeze swept up Valdez Alley. The psychic smiled, "She is gone now."

Historic records rarely record such outrages by Spanish soldiers upon the Native population. So a barbaric attack could well have taken place and we have no way of knowing it other than through psychic means.

Does the wandering lady in white still walk the alleyway trying to find to find her way home? Or did the exorcism prove successful and her spirit at long last traveled on?

Ghost Hunt: Olivas Adobe Historical Park, Ventura

Conducted by a team from Northridge University, College of Extended Learning

It was foggy that Saturday, great tendrils of mist were issuing from the nearby Pacific Ocean. I followed the road way past the green fields of crops to the old hacienda. I was no stranger here and my hands seem to almost steer the wheel by themselves. But, I was concerned about the others who would take part in the ghost hunt. They didn't know the way as I did. Did I give them good directions? Were the signs and landmarks enough for them to find this lonely adobe house on the edge of nowhere? I hoped that the high price of gas would not keep them away.

I pulled into the deserted parking lot. It was early I assured myself. They would come.

I pulled out my papers and waited. I was not disappointed . One by one the cars came. The whole team had made the trip and would look into the reports of a ghost lady wandering the grounds of the historic home. We gathered out front and gave them their instructions. Each was handed a form to fill out. On this form was a number of simple questions to see if they had ever visited the site. There was also a floor plan of the house. They were to walk the grounds and mark down places where they felt a psychic disturbance. I let them progress alone though the place. I didn't want to influence them in any way. If I should even nod or blink that might give away some of the ghostly secrets. In all such investigations, the waiting is the hardest part. In time they returned and each one had filled out their papers with many notes.

I was pleased. They marked many of the locations long rumored to be haunted! One member of the team, on the second floor, saw a figure walk past a doorway towards a window. This was telling because it was at that very window that the mysterious 'Lady in Black' has been seen for decades. Others picked up a disturbance in the kitchen and in some of the other rooms. May felt ill at ease in the ornate master bedroom. This was a place where the ghost lady has been seen and it was in this room that several members of the Olivas Family passed away. Some felt the chill that hovers in some of the rooms; it is a cold that never seems to go away even on the warmest days.

Several members of the team were drawn to the historic kitchen where a "strong female presence" was felt near the stove. After securing the papers we toured the old house. I told them where the ghost had been seen and what she looked like. Each room of the place has its own ghost story but the places they spotted were the sites where the phantom has proven herself to be most active.

Their findings, when matched to others, may give added insights to the nature of the disturbances at the Olivas Adobe. But the story doesn't end there...

After the team had disbanded, an old friend, fellow psychic investigator and archeologist Mr. Rob Wlodarski (author of The Haunted Alamo and other books on the paranormal), visited the Adobe. He had no idea I was conducting an investigation that morning. He was drawn to the old kitchen of the house and there he saw a form. *"He was standing at the railing looking toward the left. Out of the corner of my eye, I saw a figure standing near the window about 8-10 feet from me. She appeared to be dark-skinned, about 5' 4" tall, in her 30s or early 40s, wearing a dark dress, shoe-length ... it had a high collar. She was wearing a white apron, tied at the waist, and what appeared to be a white, lace doily or handkerchief on top of her head. She was facing me , holding a wooden ladle with a large spoon on the end. ... Within about five seconds, the entire vision just vanished."*

The account matches what others have seen at the house.

The reports given by the students and the chance encounter by Mr. Wlodarski give added weight to the belief that this place is indeed one of the most authentic haunted places in California. The findings confirm, in my opinion, the fact that this 1847 adobe is a haunted house equal to the Winchester Mystery House and the infamous Whaley House in San Diego.

Olivas Adobe Update

A ghostly girl appeared at Olivas Adobe to a group of nine. The members of the " lively ghosts of Ventura workshop." They got more than they bargained for when they attended the session on July 23, 2003. That night a ghost materialized before their eyes. Some of the class watched in amazement other thought it was all part of the show. "As a rule, nothing much happens at these lectures," confided Mr. Richard Senate the leader of the workshop and no stranger to a ghost himself. "This night something dramatic and unexpected occurred," he said. "I haven't seen anything this dramatic in years." The workshop highlights one of the fastest growing hobbies in the nation: Ghost Hunting. Followers of this new field of interest visit haunted sites with cameras, taper recorders and other tools to attempt to see and record supernatural events. "Amateur ghost hunters are the only ones I know of who really like pictures with fog splotches and odd blemishes because they might be pictures of ghosts," laughs Mr. Senate. "But in the last workshop, even I was taken aback, I thought I had seen it all." The workshop was held at the historic Olivas Adobe in Ventura. The first two hours talked about ghost hunting and the stories of ghosts linked to places within the city. After they learned how to investigate a site the team was taken through the old adobe home, now a museum, armed with flashlights and little more than courage. "I told them the story of the mysterious lady in black said to haunt the place," recalls Mr. Senate. "We went through the whole

"I went to the Olivas Adobe for one of the concerts they do in the summer when I saw this woman all dressed in black looking down from the balcony. I thought it was one of the volunteer ladies in a costume. When I looked away for a moment, she was gone. I learned that the ghost woman had been seen many times."

Visitor to Ventura 1999

The Olivas Adobe is located on Olivas Adobe Road near Harbor Blvd . You must visit the adobe and gift shop. The site serves as a venue for excellent music and film programs. Information 805 658-4728

house and I was wrapping things up when it happened." He asked the students to turn off their flashlights to see how really dark the place was. "We saw a glowing cloud of white light in the Children's bedroom. It seemed to move and then become the apparition of a little girl in a white night gown and cap. She stood there looking at us." Mr. Senate reports. "The girl seemed to be maybe seven or eight. Short in size, maybe 4 foot one or two. She stood there and then made a little turn around and vanished." The team rushed into the room but there was nothing there. Who the little girl is or why she was there that night is still unknown. Over the years many have seen ghosts at the old adobe. Most are described as a woman in a 1880s style black dress. Only twice before has a little girl been seen. Both times the witnesses were younger children. More investigations are needed to discover the true nature of this new apparition at the Olivas Adobe.

A new investigation captured a unique image looking in the second floor window (right.) The image resembles Mr. Nicholas Olivas (left.) Why was he looking in the window? His young daughter died at the rancho. Perhaps she is the girl seen in the bedroom.

The Earl Stanley Gardner Building is located in the heart of Downtown Ventura at the corner of Main Street and Historic California Street

VISIT

Erle Stanley Gardner Building Ghosts

The Erle Stanley Gardner Building, on the corner of California and Main Streets in Ventura, has been recognized as a historic landmark for years, first because of its distinctive style, and then because it is linked to the mystery writer, Gardner, who had an office on the third floor. The building has a little-known secret whispered about by some who have had offices there over the years, They say it's haunted.

The first account of ghostly activity was years ago, when a woman used the fourth floor as a place to store costumes for her rental agency. She said that, late at night while she was working, she would feel odd things and hear an old-style typewriter tapping. She thought it was another tenant working the wee hours of the night but when she checked, there was no one in the building!

Another man who rented an office there said that, at a set time each day, a man would pass in front of his doorway. He saw the image several times, but when he went to check there was nothing in the hall, nor did he ever hear footsteps as the man passed. He described the thing as dressed all in gray, with a narrow tie and slicked back hair. The man never looked at him, only looked down the hall. He appeared to have wire-rimmed glasses, and moved quickly down the hall. It was weeks before the tenant came to the conclusion that the odd image was a ghost.

The most bizarre event took place late one night when a man claimed to have heard the distinct sounds of a party going on. The music was old-style big band sounds of the 1930s, the voices and laughter belonged to a large group of men and women having a good time. Walking down the hall he saw, through the glass in a window, a group of people wearing paper hats on their heads and holding wine glasses in their hands. When he first saw the party going on, he had to smile, and turned to leave them to celebrate in private. Then he realized that when he saw them there was absolutely no sound! He turned and saw that the party now was silent when before it was very loud when he walked down the hallway. He then took time to examine the odd goings on and noticed that the dresses and hairstyles on the women were not right--they were more the styles of sixty years ago. The men were all dressed in suits and ties, with clothes that were out of style. The witness heard a sound, glanced back, and saw nothing in the hallway behind him. When he looked back the office was dark and the phantom party gone.

Other strange events seemed to be focused on the first floor that was used for decades as a bank. For a number of years it has been an upscale furniture store. Before the present antique store moved in, when it was under different management, I was called in because of a number of ghostly happenings at the place.

Employees complained of loud screams as they were locking up. Still others said that large objects had seemingly moved by themselves late at night. Was it pranksters, or was the old building haunted? Though we conducted a séance at the building late one night, we were never able to pin down any facts to prove the question of ghosts one way or the other.

So the question must be addressed, is the Erle Stanley Gardner Building haunted? Perhaps. Is it haunted by the ghost of old Erle, perhaps still concocting a new mystery plot long after he has left this earthly plane? There is not one bit of evidence that this is so and, to date, none of the reported phenomena can be linked to Mr. Gardner. But dynamic people, people driven to make their mark upon the world, do seem to come back in spirit form.

Erle Stanley Gardner
(1889-1970)
American detective novelist, born in Malden, Massachusetts. His numerous novels are notable for their fast action and revelations of legal ingenuity, the latter due in part to Gardner's work for more than 20 years as an attorney. The character of lawyer-detective Perry Mason appeared in more than 80 of Gardner's novels.

The Ghost of Rosa

She haunts the restaurant on Santa Clara Street (today the Landmark 78 Steak House.) They say Rosa took her own life when she became pregnant and her Italian lover moved on. Now she is sen in a long dress in the Ladies Rest Room! She also has a very long neck and white face!

This fine restaurant is reputed to be haunted by a ghost that wanders the upper floor and staircase. It is said to be a girl named Rosa who hung herself in despair at the turn of the century. The woman is felt many times in the Ladies Room of the Restaurant. Many have seen this specter in her long dress. One witness noticed that the apparition's neck is unnaturally long and twisted, an ominous reminder of her suicide! Many sightings are just before closing late at night and many of the sightings are seen of the women in the mirror! One visitor to the restaurant's ladies room attempted to converse with the phantom and had the spirit "walk" right through her sending icy chills down her back.

Stylish old building, great menu and warm service. The Landmark No. 78 Restaurant is located at 211 East Santa Clara.

The Victorian Rose Inn

The old Church stands in gothic splendor on Main Street near Downtown Ventura. It was built on this site in 1888 when the streets were made of dirt and worshipers came in horse and buggy. Then it was surrounded by empty fields. It served the town as a protestant church for many years becoming a landmark with its 90 foot tall spire. But, even long ago there were whispered stories that the place was haunted.

There was a tale that a ghostly singer inhabited the choir loft. There she would sing her shrill soprano songs on moon lit nights. There was also the story of a ghostly minister who walked the halls and haunted the pulpit, ready to give just one more sermon and save one more soul.

The church has been transformed into a bed and breakfast Inn but from all accounts the ghosts are still there and, if anything they are more active than ever. Visitors tell of hearing singing coming from the room that was once the loft. A woman was seen walking back right through a wall. A team was called into investigate the five room Inn. They came away convinced that several ghosts haunt the old church. The woman in the loft and the phantom man in black--a preacher who seems to still desire to help people. One woman woke up in the middle of the night to find her bed madly vibrating. At first she thought it was some sort of machine built in to give the guests a good nights sleep. When she tried to turn it off or unplug it--she found nothing there. Another woman spending the night at the place felt a phantom touch her. Another saw a full apparition appear next to the bathroom doorway in the "Time's Remembered" room. A seance was held in the place that seemed to communicate with one of the ghosts who said he was a man of the cloth still working to reach sinners and bring them to the light. The ghost hunt was a success in that it confirmed the old stories were true and the Victorian Rose is indeed haunted. Some of the ghosts seem to have moved on over the years only to be replaced with new ones--the most recent sighting? A man dressed as a 19th Century farmer. The Inn is well worth a visit and a must for all who would seek a chance to "sleep with a ghost"!

Last weekend, I spent three nights (at the Victorian Rose Bed & Breakfast) and experienced some curious events. The most interesting event took place on Sunday...about 3 or 4 am. I was sitting on the couch in the large central lobby area when I heard the loud, unmistakable sound of a woman in high heels walking into the room. These footsteps came from the main entry way (directly under the steeple) and continued walking south through the room. As you know, the room is full of antique furniture. The steady tempo of the footsteps made me realize that the lasdy that I heard was walking a straight line and could not be turning corners around the furniture in the room...I began to have a hunch that this might really be a ghost. Those footsteps were very loud and easy to hear. The tempo of the footsteps was fast. I heard them for a full 30 seconds. I swear this is absolutely true.

Bill C____________

Victorian Rose Bed & Breakfast
Beautiful Inn, delightful hosts. 896 E. Main, Ventura.

The Ghosts of the Pierpont Inn

The Old Inn has stood upon the bluff overlooking the pier and ocean since 1910. It has become a landmark in Ventura where dining is still an experience. Over the decades many famous people have visited this place. A short list would include writer Erle Stanley Gardner, cowboy star Roy Rogers, baseball legend Babe Ruth, actress Jane Fonda, director Cecil B. DeMille and even President George Bush and first lady Barbara. But some visitors, so it seems, continue on as non-paying guests ghosts!

Many of the stories first came to light during recent restoration and re-construction. This is common in many haunted places, changes seem to bring out the afterimages of the past almost as if they are some supernatural DVD played back to people with the gift (or curse) of psychic insight. Most of the encounters are friendly enough.

Many of the ghostly events have taken place in the dinning room area. One hostess was working late at night, and went into the kitchen. There are a pair of swinging door reminiscent of the sorts of door one might find in a western saloon. She pushed them open to get herself a cup of hot coffee. Behind her she her the doors opening and shutting with the distinct clatter that accompanies such movement. She looked back to see who was coming only to see no one there and the doors violently swinging back and forth.

Not long after that one of the servers was near the same location and observed a woman dressed in an early 20th Century costume. She was wearing a satin dress, long white gloves, a hat with a feather and an umbrella. He rubbed his eyes and when he opened them again the apparition was gone!

Still another encounter came in the fall of 2000 when a young houseman came in to clean one of the banquet rooms after an event. He was waiting for instructions on what to do when he observed a couple enter into the room, cross the chamber and sit down at the table where he was working. He reported that the man and woman were both fully transparent! He left the room shaking.

Even the dishwasher has encountered one of the many Pierpont ghosts. He was leaving the Inn late one night after finishing his shift. As he approached his car, parked in the lower lot, he saw a woman dancing next to the trash cans. She was waving her arms and jumping high into the air seemingly completely unaware of his presence. An interesting fact is that this image, like that couple, was also transparent! In a few moments the dancing woman seemed to vanish into thin air.

But ghosts are also found in a place always full of spirits, the bar. In 2001 two visitors were at the bar at about 10 pm. One of the men looked over to an alcove and saw something moving. It was sort of a mist that formed three ribbons floating above the table. He alerted his friend to what he had seen but it was gone. The mist had vanished. The bartender remembers that the man was ashen white while telling what happened next, the supernatural events were not over for these two. As they left, they discovered that the inside of their car reeked of the scent of flowers almost as if a funeral had taken place inside their car. Checking outside of the car, the odd sweet smell it was only in the car.

Some of the most bizarre events have taken place on the second floor, in a section of the Inn yet to be renovated. These former rooms are now used as offices by the hotel management. One woman, was working late designing a new menu when she heard the distinct sound of the ruffling. The kind of sound a stiff taffeta petticoat might make. There was no one there! As the odd sound passed her by, there was a cool breeze of rushing air. She checked, all the doors and windows were closed.

Another employee was working at a copy machine in the same area on the second floor. She looked up and saw one of the managers walking down the hall. Holding his hand was a little girl in a fancy dress. The girl was all smiles and giggles. The man and girl went into the manager's office. She called out to ask who the girl was, believing it to be his grand daughter or something. He stepped out surprised he didn't know what she was talking about. "There is no little girl here" he said. Later the witness identified the child from an old photograph. The apparition was that of a daughter of the former owner. The picture had been taken in the 1930s!

These are but a few of the many stories of ghosts at the historic Pierpont Inn. As Cynthia Thompson of the Inn observed: " Most of our 'visitors' from another time seem to be friendly. It appears they have had such a good time here at the Pierpont , they simply don't want to leave."

The Pierpont Inn in the early days.

The Pierpont Inn offers lovely accommodations and a restaurant really worth visiting! 550 Sanjon Road, Ventura

"The theater at the High School (Ventura) is haunted by the ghost of a man named Toby. He likes to make sounds and, like, move things.... he's really not evil or anything.... he's just there."
- Ventura High School student

"I don't really believe in ghosts but I did have something strange happen to me at Foster Library (in Ventura). I was looking for a book in the reference section and felt a tap on my shoulder. It was a hard, almost enough to hurt. When I looked there was nothing there."

- Ventura resident

The Lady in White of Cemetery Park

The ghost is dressed all in white, some feel she died before her wedding day. She has a large picture hat and drifts over the former cemetery calling out peoples names! She seems to be looking for someone, but who? Why does she float over the grass of the park in the wee hours of the morning? Perhaps she, like others, are thought to protest the removal of the tombstones in 1969. The markers were removed from the old cemetery and pitched into the sea!

Haunted Saticoy Road

I received a letter from a citizen of Ventura..

I was recently told a story and wondered if you had any background information. My friend Candy told me one night she was driving on Saticoy Road, coming towards Telegraph, when she saw a young man with brown hair wearing a red shirt and blue jeans, standing in the middle of the road....she didn't have enough time to stop without hitting him so she flashed her brights..then he was gone. No one else in the car saw it so they didn't believe her but I found it kind of interesting so I thought I would see if you knew anything about it...Thanks

(Many sightings of a phantom hitchhiker have been seen on this road over the years. **RS**)

The Ghosts of Bard Hospital

The 1902 period hospital was abandoned for years and had the appearance of a traditional haunted site. Dr. Bard was the first doctor in the city and he dedicated the hospital to his mother. Dr. Bard's brother, Senator Thomas R. Bard, is memorialized in Oxnard. He has a building and street named after him.

The first patient in the Bard Hospital was the doctor himself. He was also the first person to die there, too. He was cremated and his ashes placed in a beverage bottle and then hidden in the hospital.

In it's prime, it was a modern facility with two wards and fourteen private rooms and an operating room on each floor.

I had collected many stories of ghosts visible in windows but did not visit the hospital until one of my ghost hunting classes went there on a field trip. At that time, the building was owned by the inventors workshop and most of the structure was unoccupied.

We gathered on Sunday at 10:00 and went right to work. Psychic Nadean Peterson took the lead and described a number of psychic impressions. Nadean saw a little girl who died because her legs were crushed by a water wagon. There is a stern nurse who walks the halls of the second floor as she holds a lamp. The man who had the hospital built is amongst those who haunts the site. Nadean described him as a rotund man with large sideburns He smokes a pipe, drinks a little too much and smells of both.

Several others in the group sensed a number of psychic impressions, but I did not expect myself to have any. I separated from the group and went into the most eery room in the building. It is adjacent to what was the morgue, I was in the brick basement.

I felt a distinct chill race down my back as entered a small dark room. The room became cold and I felt the presence of evil. I was held in the room by the force.

There was a small flash of light then a shadow appeared. It took the form of a man, but only his face and torso were visible. He had a scar on the right side of his face. This man seemed to have been one of the hospital employees for he was wearing a white lab coat. It's possible that is was the specter of Dr. Bard himself. This vision lasted only seconds then the ghost melted into the brick wall.

A strong sense of greed , envy and pain remained. Perhaps these emotions trap him there. He seem to resent my presence, and all at once I felt I must leave the basement.

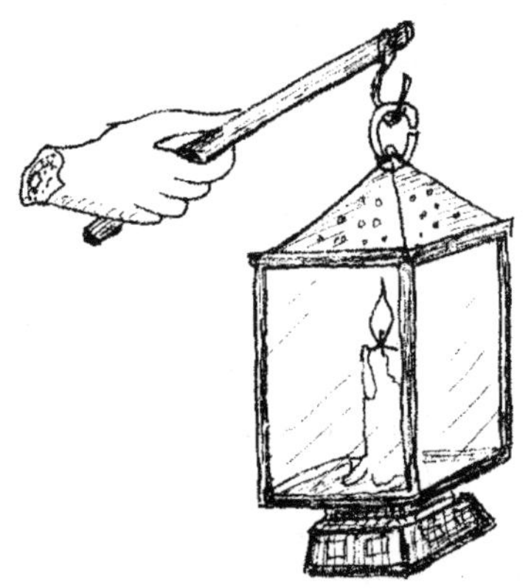

"Ventura is just filled with ghosts,
I saw one at the old cemetery park one night.
It was like....a floating ball of yellow light
that moved over the ground.....
about three feet. I was silent. Then it was gone."

- Long time Ventura resident

The Door to the Spirit World in an Art Gallery

The *Things from Heaven* store in downtown Ventura locals know as the *Angel Store.* It's a good name for the place because it sells all things angelic. The Main Street shop has been open since 1995 and almost from the first, strange, supernatural things have happened there. Perhaps the most amazing events occur in the art gallery in the rear of the store. Remarkably people claimed that they have seen the spirits of dead relatives, or even gotten messages from the great beyond. Some believe that this place is a sort of vortex, or door to the 'other side'. The Greeks believed such spots existed, and called them Psychomanteums. Mr. Richardson has compiled a list of the odd events in his book *Andy Lakey's Psychomanteum,* and a new planned book on the phenomena. These are but a few of the spiritual encounters at his store.

One Sunday afternoon in February, our employee Jane came running to the front of the store to get me. She was frantic with excitement. She motioned to me with her hand and said, "Keith! Keith! Come quick. It's starting to happen."

"What's happening?" I demanded impatiently.

"The psychomanteum!" She shouted. "It's becoming active again. You've got to see what's going on."

I walked briskly behind Jane as she led me into the gallery of Andy Lakey's art. There in front of me was a six-year-old girl named Dakota with her hand over one of Lakey's paintings. The little girl appeared to be in a trance.

After a few moments Dakota opened her eyes and looked at her mother, a woman with short blonde hair who appeared to be in her late twenties, and said, "Mommy, Mommy, I feel like I was touched by Jesus. I saw Grandma Judy. I was holding her hand."

Dakota's mother began to weep openly. "Oh my God," she said, "Her grandma died last year. They were always very close."

I stepped in at this point and asked the distraught woman a few questions, "Have you ever been to our store before?"

"No," she replied. "I didn't even know your store existed until today. We just stumbled upon it by accident. We're not from around here; we're from Ridgecrest, California (a city about two-hours northeast of Ventura)."

"Have you ever heard of Andy Lakey?" I asked.

"No, not until just now when Jane showed us his art. What's going on here anyway?" She demanded.

"Well," I said, "This may seem a little hard to believe, but from time to time people who come into this gallery of Andy Lakey's art see departed loved ones and get messages from the other side. We think that is what just happened with your daughter."

The woman looked bewildered.

I then asked, "Would it be possible for me to talk to Dakota about what she saw so I can further document what's going on in our gallery?"

The woman thought for a moment and then nodded, "Yes."

I went to the front of the store and got a yellow legal pad to take notes on. When I returned to the gallery, I walked over to Dakota and said, "What did you see?"

After I asked this question the young girl fell silent and ran over to her mother, held onto her leg and refused to speak. I looked at Jane and said, "I don't think she wants to talk to me. She seems to like you. Maybe she will tell us what she saw, if you ask the questions."

Jane walked over to Dakota and began to do something that greatly concerned me. She asked her very unscientific leading questions.

"Did you see your grandmother in heaven?" She asked.

"No!" Replied Dakota. "My grandma Judy was in a park in Chicago. We used to go there a lot together."

"Were there angels with your grandmother?" She asked.

"No!" Dakota responded, "Only my grandma was an angel, she had beautiful white wings and wore a long white gown that shimmered. The only other things I saw with her were her little dogs."

Dakota named several animals she saw and then her mother, who was standing with us sobbed and said, "Those were the little dogs she had that died."

Jane then continued her questioning. "Dakota, did your grandmother tell you anything?"

"Yes, she did," she answered. "My grandma said she loved me and that we'd be together again in heaven one day."

Dakota's mother took me aside and said, "This is all very traumatic, and Dakota doesn't know it, but her grandma Judy committed suicide six months ago. My husband and I are strong Christians and we've been taught to believe that you go to Hell if you kill yourself. It's really reassuring to know that this isn't true. I'm really happy to know that grandma Judy's in heaven and happy with her little dogs."

Another strange event took place in December.

It was a crazy December's day at our store. The Sunday before Christmas our store is always busy, but this day was especially frantic. Maybe this is why the forces from the other side seemed more active than ever in our gallery of Andy Lakey art.

About 3:00 p.m. a rather striking woman walked into the store. She appeared to be in her early forties and had dark black hair and deep brown eyes. She said her name was Marilyn.

"I don't know why I came into your store," she said. "I've never been here before. I didn't know this store even existed. I just felt drawn to come in."

"A lot of people tell me this," I said. "Did you find a place to park right in front of our store?" I asked.

"Yes." She nodded with a surprised look on her face, "How did you know?"

"It happens here all the time." I said. "We don't know why for sure, but generally when this happens, there is a good reason for you being here."

Marilyn smiled and said, "You're right, I do have a reason for being in an angel store. My mother passed away last week from complications of a long term illness."

"I'm sorry to hear about your mother," I said, "I lost my mother last year, and I know how hard it can be."

Marilyn then looked at me a little cautiously and said, " I haven't told anyone this. They'd think I'm crazy, but I think I can trust you. The night of my mother's death I dreamt that I accompanied her to heaven."

"What was it like?" I asked.

"It was beautiful," Marilyn said. "We walked down a path lined with the most beautiful bright colored flowers, grass and trees. They glowed like neon. My mother was holding my hand. It was really beautiful. I remember when I stepped on the path it would change colors under my feet. I was awakened from this dream by the ringing of my telephone. It was the hospital calling to tell me my mother had died."

I looked at Marilyn reassuringly and said, "What happened to you is not abnormal. The majority of the people who lose loved ones see them again as spirits. It's just all the dispirited people in the psychiatric and medical professions that are making us think we are crazy when this happens. For millions of years we as humans have experienced this sort of thing, and it has helped us. It has just been in this century that we've been told these experiences aren't normal."

I made a gesture to Marilyn with my hand and said, "Come with me into the gallery of art by Andy Lakey. You'll see for yourself that what I'm saying is true."

Marilyn followed me through the door at the back of my store into the gallery.

"Have you heard of this artist?" I asked.

"No," she replied.

I told Marilyn Andy's story and described his mission to paint two thousand Angel paintings by the year 2000. The story and the art fascinated Marilyn.

"You can touch these paintings," I said. "But if you put your hand about an inch above them, some people feel something coming off them. Try it."

Marilyn cautiously put her hand over the painting. "Wow! There's energy in those paintings!" she said. She went around the gallery trying all of the paintings and getting similar results.

As we stood there, my employee, Jane, entered the gallery with a family of four, a father, mother and two daughters. Jane told the family about Andy's art and had them run their hands above it. Their younger daughter Isabelle, a Hispanic girl in her early teens with braided pigtails, put her hands over one of the paintings, and closed her eyes.

A few seconds later, Jane called me over to her side. "Oh, my God Keith! I think it's happening again. Look at that girl," she said.

Isabelle was in a catatonic trance-like state. Her eyes were closed, but they fluttered beneath her eyelids.

"I think you're right." I said, "There really seems to be something going on here."

After a few moments Isabelle came back to consciousness. "Did you see anything?" I asked.

"Yes," said Isabelle. "I saw my mother, she was reaching out to me."

Isabelle then put her hand on a second painting, went into the same state and when she opened her eyes again said, "I was holding my mother's hand."

Her father, who was standing next to me, said, "Isabelle is our foster child. She just came to live with us."

The family stayed in the gallery a few more moments, then went to the front of the store and related Isabelle's experience to my wife, Francesca. "When did your mother die?" asked Francesca.

"My mother isn't dead," replied Isabelle.

The family left the store after making their purchases and Francesca went to the back of the store, where I was still with Marilyn, to tell me of her concern. "No one has ever seen a living loved one come out of the painting," She said.

"This is really odd," I said.

Jane entered the gallery. We told her of our concern. How could someone see a living person come out of the paintings?

"Didn't Isabelle's foster father tell you what happened?" she said. They just got Isabelle as a foster child because both of her parents were killed.

No one has told her yet of the tragedy. They brought her here today to help her deal with the news when she finally receives it.

Events keep happening at the Things From Heaven Store. Is it really a doorway into the next world? Who can say? It is built on what was once part of the Old Mission San Buenaventura complex. There was an Native American village near by long ago and the Chumash tribe was (and still are) a spiritual people. Maybe there is something on this piece of land, activated by the mystic paintings and spiritual content of the store, that unlocks the psychic gifts we all carry within our souls. Visit the place and see if you encounter the unknown.

Haunted Plaza Park

Ghosts do not need buildings to haunt. Some of the most haunted places on planet Earth are just spaces, open fields and such. One such location in Ventura, known for its ghosts, is a simple park in the center of the old town section. I had heard rumors of ghosts there for many years. My first informant was a young boy scout who told me of the ghost man of the "hanging tree". As no hangings were ever conducted in the park and the only great tree in the area was a Morton Bay fig planted in 1874, I dismissed the story as a product of an overactive imagination. That was until the night I saw the thing with my own eyes.

I was driving home after a dinner at the Landmark 78 restaurant (also a haunted site) when I reached the intersection of Santa Clara and Chestnut Streets. It was perhaps 9:30 at night when this took place. I saw a man pass in front of my car against the light. I almost hit the form causing me to apply the brakes. The man didn't look at me but I saw him distinctly in my headlights. He was wearing a beard, a black tailcoat, vest and a tall, Lincoln style stove pipe hat of the 19th Century. He looked very real as he rushed on to the sidewalk towards the huge fig tree. It was then that the apparition started to come apart. He had nothing below the knees! It seconds it vanished, the top hat the last to go.

The whole thing didn't last five seconds.

Who was the figure? Why was it rushing across the street? Being a ghost, he didn't need to worry about being hit by a car. I learned that I wasn't the first or the last to encounter the ghosts of Plaza Park.

It was first designated as a park in 1866, when the town was incorporated. At first it was little more than a field where locals tethered their milk cows, and they even planted potatoes here once. Finally, green grass, trees and a gazebo were placed on the park site. Here the surviving members of the "Grand Army of the Republic" would meet to remember the Civil War.

Political figures came to give speeches and brass bands played. Once, it is said, John Philip Sousa's Band played here to a park packed with residents; and President McKinley spoke to some 3,000 before his fateful assassination. Could the ghost be linked to the colorful and rich history of the park? Could he be a local businessman rushing to a brass concert or an aspiring political figure hurrying to give his speech?

Another story came to me that might explain the ghost. It is a romantic tale that sounds more like folklore than fact. I have read many such tales in locations all over the world that sound something like this. A man loved a woman in old Ventura. She was from an important family and he was poor. He professed his love to the young woman and vowed he would find his fortune in the world and return for her. He left Ventura for San Francisco. A few letters came, then nothing. In time, she feared he was dead. She married a local man of substance, and they built a home not far from the park. At last, the young man returned, now rich from his travels in the Far East and the Gold Rush. He was shocked to find his sweetheart married! He moved to Ventura and would see his love only as she strolled in Plaza Park each day. They say that their ghosts appear walking towards one another; she, with feathered hat and Victorian dress from one corner, he in his coat and top hat from the opposite. They slowly walk towards one another but vanish before they can meet. A great story, but is it true? Some have seen a woman in the park wearing the fancy clothing of the Victorian era. Others have seen a man as well. So, perhaps the story of the doomed lovers has some basis in fact. The names of the two are shrouded in the mist of history but, perhaps, through supernatural means they could be united in some afterlife?

Brent Street Ghost Dog

I woke up out of a Saturday afternoon nap to the sounds of a dog's toenails on the polished hardwood floors. Anyone who has owned a dog will know what I mean. The only problem was - I didn't have a dog! I was home alone, or so I thought. I got up and looked down the hallway towards the living room. I saw the head of a large dog peering around the corner, glaring at me. I could see its ears, nose and one of its forepaws. As I looked, it backed away out of my line of sight. I thought that my wife must have left the front door open, and some stray or neighbors dog had some in seeking food. I slowly padded in stocking feet down the hall, not knowing what to expect. When I got to the living room, I found the door locked. There was no dog around. I searched the whole house from top to bottom, but there was not a sign of the hound. I almost wrote the whole thing off as a dream except for the odd tingle on the back of my neck when I saw the thing. It was the same thing I felt when encountering a ghost.

My stepson later told me he too had seen the "doggie". I had not shared the story of my encounter with him because he was a young boy at the time, and might become frightened if he thought the house was haunted. He said he saw the dog two or three times, and it was a good dog that just wanted to play. Perhaps it was just coincidence, I thought except that I do not believe in coincidences. I was rushing to work the next time I saw the phantom dog. I was alone in the house and walking down the hall when I looked back. I don't know why I looked. I know I didn't hear anything or have a reason to glance back--I just did. I saw the dog in the hall looking at me. It was the same creature. But, here is the strange part. It was only half a dog. The apparition stopped midway. The thing had no back end or rear feet! This time the dog just vanished away. This was too bizarre even for me. My wife, Debbie, also encountered the dog but, it was from her that we learned the story behind the odd apparition. A young man came to the house one day. He told my wife he had lived in the house before we rented the place. On an impulse, Debbie asked if he had a dog. He told her he did but, just before he moved out, the dog ran out the front door and into the street. A truck rolled over the animal crushing its back and hips. The big loving dog died in its master's arms. This might explain why there was just a half of the dog visible. The dog was seen several more times until we moved to another place. I always wonder if the animal still haunts the house on Brent Street, Ventura, or perhaps it has moved on to whatever afterlife exists for our loyal pets.

The Ghost Lady of the Cross

On the hill overlooking the city of Ventura is a tall cross. The venerable Fray Juniper Serra placed it on the hill back in 1782. Many legends swirl around the old cross. There are tales of a lost treasure chest bound with iron bands, a strange murder and, naturally, a ghost story. I love ghost stories, especially when they might be true!

A woman all dressed in white is said to haunt the area around the cross. Her dress is like that of a Victorian nightgown. Her hair is raven black and flowing almost to her waist. The most striking feature of this apparition is that she has NO FACE. There is just a blank spot where a face should be. This is common with many reports of Latina ghosts. The tale goes back to the days when the Mission flourished in the early years of the 19th Century. A Spanish soldier lured a beautiful Native Chumash girl to the cross late one night. Here he assaulted her and, to keep her from telling the padres of his act, he strangled her and buried her near the cross. The cross would become her tombstone. She was listed the next day as a "runaway" and search parties were sent out to find her. They never did, and her name was taken off the Mission lists. But, her murderer didn't prosper. He was haunted by her figure in his dreams. He requested a transfer to a different mission, but whereever he went, his nights were filled with the faceless ghost until, drunk and feverish from sleeplessness, he took his pistol and shot himself. As he deserved, he is buried in an unmarked grave, on unhallowed grounds, in Santa Barbara.

A story, it is true, but people have seen the ghost woman! One woman told me that a carload of her friends were visiting the cross one warm summer night. The view from the site is both impressive and beautiful; a must-see for visitors. As they drove up the narrow road, a woman in a long white dress with flowing hair stepped in front of the car. They could see through the apparition! And they all noticed that she had no face. The image turned and vanished. Others have seen her drifting near the cross itself. For many years, the cross was a sort of lovers lane with the locals and some of the strangest stories came from couples that saw the faceless ghost lady "looking" at them through the car windows. Many of the witnesses were Latinos and Latinas. The sightings always took place in the hour after midnight. Perhaps guilt was behind the sightings. Every time the ghost lady is seen it ends any romantic tryst, almost at once. Most of the time, it is the young woman who sees the thing. Some say the ghostly Native American woman comes as a warning to alert women to men who are not true to their love. She acts to prevent women from sharing her fate at that hands of scoundrels. A story only? Not to those who have seen the ghost lady of the cross.

"People have seen ghosts around here for years. There's a ghost up at the cross. I have never seen her myself but my sister did." - Ventura Resident

The Ghosts of the Duchess III

The yacht is rumored to have once been the property of gangland kingpin Al "Scarface" Capone. Some say he went out on the great lakes in the boat on "fishing trips," and on each occasion fewer people came back. The vessel is now moored in Ventura Harbor and, if all the eyewitness accounts are true--it is a very haunted boat.

Research failed to bring up a connection to "Big Al," but it did list a number of unsavory owners from gunrunners, to cultists and Neo-Nazi's. The old *Duchess III* has seen a great deal of life in her years. The 60 foot yacht is wooden hulled and was launched in the 1920s. She served at a prison launch in Washington State, and as a hospital ship in Alaska before taking on more sinister owners. Some of these may still be aboard as ghosts.

I became aware of the vessel's ghostly reputation when I met a man restoring the craft.

"You want ghosts," he said, *"you ought to come on my boat, its full of them!"* Doug F.___________ told me of many strange events that he and others had seen, from apparitions to things moving about by themselves. Once, he informed me, a set of wires came alive and tried to strangle someone! He was understandably having trouble finding people to work on the boat.

The events he listed caused me to set up a number of investigations. I had my wife come to the old boat, and she felt that at least two ghosts walked the decks, a man who was a murderer, and a woman named "Jo," who might have been a dancer or "gun moll." A TV team from KEYT-TV, Santa Barbara came down and did an investigation of the *Duchess III*. It became a segment picked up by the whole ABC network as a sort of filler for the news. The owner tried to sell the boat with little success. One woman who came aboard felt icy hands running through her long hair as she walked on the deck. Her friend saw her hair rise up in an unnatural way as she let out a whimper and left the boat, vowing to never return.

The owner lost the boat and another stepped in. She was taken into the yards and her hull restored. Still, late at night people at the harbor would see lights in the portholes, even when there was no one on board. More owners came and went, and for a time she found herself as a sort of attraction, with tours and ghost stories. But, each owner reported strange manifestations on the yacht. The most common: footsteps pacing the deck when there was no one there. A second ghost hunt was set up to determine whom the ghost (or ghosts) was and why they continued to haunt. Debbie refused to attend this time.

"I'll never set foot on that boat again" she vowed. "There is something evil and depressing on that boat. They should just take it out to sea and give her a decent funeral."

Another psychic came forward and now with a full group we went to the boat. Again, this team found evidence of two ghosts, a man and a woman. The man was angry and negative, the woman sad and lonely. While attempting to contact the ghostly man in the cold forward cabin, I asked the spirit to show himself. He didn't. I then asked if he would do something to prove he was there. We all waited in the near darkness for a few moments. Then it came--three loud raps on the hull. The sound came from below our feet, from below the waterline! Unless there was a skin-diver or playful dolphin about, the raps might have been the mysterious ghost man. One tale about the yacht that interests many is that there is a treasure hidden on the boat. A sack of cash left there by the gangsters. The angry ghost, a gangster "Capo", guards the treasure for his boss, Big Al. Perhaps the legend is just a story or, maybe, if there was a treasure it was long since removed. The ghost, so it seems, didn't get the memo, and still watches over the missing loot.

My findings, and that of the team confirmed that the yacht is haunted and the ghosts active.

Supernatural events still happen on the *Duchess III* and the present owners plan to write a book on the many strange things that happen there.

It is now located at Ventura Harbor, Spinnaker Lane, Ventura, and is a private vessel.

Follow Harbor Boulevard to Ventura Harbor (Spinnaker Lane) for interesting shopping, breakfast, lunch or dinner and ghost hunting of course!

Ortega Adobe, 215 West Main Street
Open daily to the public, free admission.
Main Street just west of the Mission San Buenaventura.

The Ghost of the Ortega Adobe

Ghosts cling to places that they loved in life. Perhaps that is why spirits haunt a historic building in downtown Ventura.

It stands near the Von's Market Center on Ventura's Main Street. Few visit the place now, even though it is a recognized historic landmark. The small three-room adobe house is the birthplace of the Ortega Chili Company--established here in 1897. The humble building is much older--built by Emigdio Ortega in 1857. Maps made in 1853 indicate an adobe building on the site, so the age of the place may well go back further.

Few visit the spot, now a museum, and now only memories walk its rooms. But, if one takes the time to visit the place, they may well be rewarded with a phantom encounter.

One witness saw a ghostly man wearing a derby hat standing near one of the pillars of the porch. Others tell of feeling an icy cold spot float past or through them as they look in the side doorway. Still others say they hear a phantom guitar playing softly in the sala room.

The only sightings of a ghost report a man with a derby hat, but psychics believe that the resident specter is that of a woman. The building has had a colorful past. Once it was the home of the large Ortega Family. Members of the family did die in the house. Mr. Ortega had married a Chumash Native American woman (Native Americans are many times very psychic). The house was once a Chili Factory, a saloon, a Chinese Laundry, a pottery shop, a Speakeasy, a Veterans of Foreign Wars Hall, an employment office, a police station and lastly a Boys and Girls hall. Perhaps one of these incarnations has left behind the ghost (or ghosts). A great deal of history has passed before these walls and some, so it seems, has lingered on. It is well worth a visit, and if you do, keep one eye open for a flash of light or your ears tuned to the notes of a Spanish Guitar.

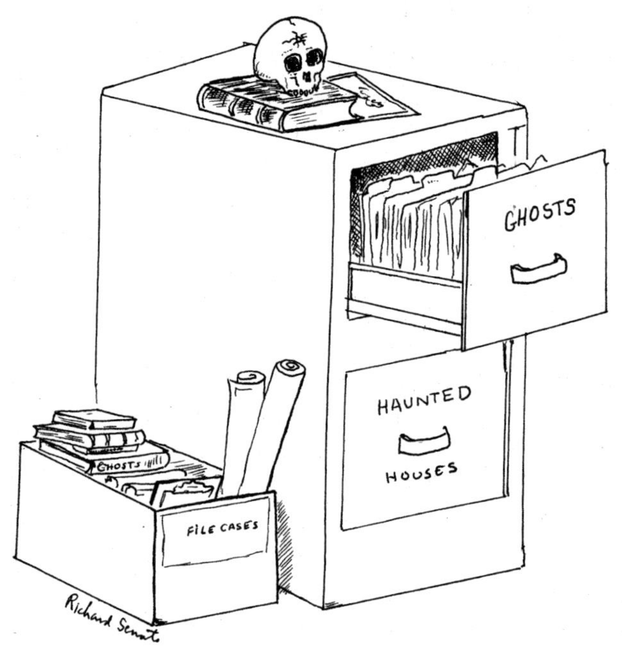
GHOSTS
HAUNTED
HOUSES
GHOSTS
FILE CASES
Richard Senate

The Ghost Hunter's Case Book

These accounts are by two members of a team that I took to a haunted house on Ocean Avenue in Ventura. They may have been more interested in reporting on each other than the ghosts in the house. It is interesting how different people can have different experiences while ghost hunting. The names have been changed to protect the innocent.

INVESTIGATION AT A HAUNTED HOUSE
by Bill H. Katzen

Mr. Richard Senate asked me to come along with him and his team to investigate the paranormal happenings at the Ocean Avenue house in Ventura, California, on the night of August 13th. I have known of Mr. Senate's work for the last five years but it was only after several mysterious events happened to me that I gave credibility to the notion that there could be ghosts in this world.

We arrived at 7:43 and parked near the 1950s style tract home. I noticed that the lawn wasn't well taken care of and toys and a tricycle were scattered on the driveway. The house was on the inside, messy as well. A man and woman were waiting in the house and two of three children were watching a cartoon on the television. We were invited in. Senate immediately began asking questions about the paranormal events the family had called to report.

They events were as follows:

1. *A table that rattled on one leg late at night.*
2. *A large picture of a farm house the came off the wall and landed nine feet from where it once hung.*
3. *A bowl that came from a counter to the living room floor.*
4. *An odd sound like tapping at the kitchen window.*
5. *A light that seemed to appear in the living room (seen twice)*
6. *A tall shadow seen standing at the doorway of the kitchen.*
7. *Dog acting funny (barking and whimpering) in back yard.*

Senate discounted the story of the dog and the image of the shadow form as it took place after the family was already convinced the house was "haunted." The children's imaginations ran rampant and they were reporting all sorts of supernatural events. The best evidence seems to be the picture coming off the wall. That event was witnessed by both adults as well as an aunt who was a dinner guest. The picture was on the wall during dinner - 6 to 6:40 then seen on the floor at about 8:20. The picture had no marks on the frame and the nail that held it to the wall wasn't bent in any way. Senate tried to knock the picture down as it hung on the wall without success. It seems that the picture has to be lifted up to be removed from the wall nail. The picture was undamaged, and was found leaning against the wall it had to have been removed with great care and placed on the floor. All of the people were in the back yard at the time so there wasn't anyone who could have moved the picture.

The case can be seen either of two ways:

A) Fraud - The picture moved by one of the adults at some point, or

B) Poltergeist - The picture was moved by a phantom for reason or reasons unknown.

Senate took the report and had a "psychic" feel the "vibrations" in the house. This "madam-psychic" felt that a ghostly boy haunted the house and caused the events. This didn't match the witnesses, who say they saw the shadow of an adult. She even said that the boy's spirit was holding her hand and that she would "lead the boy to the light." This psychic person then walked away as if she was holding someone's hand, out to the backyard. I stayed behind to watch the way the family reacted while the rest of the team went to "release the spirit of the little boy." The wife looked serious and concerned, but the father seemed to be snickering as if he had put something over on the ghost hunters. I took EM (electro-magnetic) readings and found a space about three feet square in the kitchen where the readings did shoot up. There were so many items in the kitchen that might account for this, the PC was also located near the kitchen and could have caused a false reading. The "psychic" said the house was now free of spirits, but I didn't feel anything different in the home.

We all left at 11:38 and recorded our findings. Mr. Senate was convinced that there was something in the house but whatever it was, it was not the cause of all the events. He believed it was a poltergeist linked to the 13 year old son (who hated the picture that was moved.) He politely discounted many of the things the "psychic" said. (I did see him roll his eyes as this woman blathered on about the ghost boy.) He is too nice to say anything negative about people, but I felt she added nothing to the investigation.

If the stories told by the family are true, the house has a common poltergeist. If not, the investigation was a waste of time and confirmed that the ghost was the result of over-active imaginations. Don't get me wrong. I believe ghosts really do exist. I just doubt there was one at this house we visited. Mr. Senate told me to be more open minded - I told him to open his eyes. Richard, I am sure you will not put this in your newsletter.

- Bill H. Katzen

HOUSE GHOST ON OCEAN AVENUE
By Madam Helen

Mr. Senate called me and asked for a report on the visit to the house on Ocean Avenue, I was so glad that I could come and help Michael to the next world. He was the ghost that was in the house. All he wanted to do was to play with the other children in the house. I could feel all of his confusion the moment I walked into the place.

Mr. Senate was always helpful and so understanding of the problems the family were having with the ghost. There was a Mr. Bill that was always running this way and that, with his strange little machines that were going beep-beep-beep. He is a believer who tried hard not to believe. He was always getting in my way just as I was trying to focus on the poor spirit trapped in the house.

The spirit was a little boy who died there long ago after a fall from a horse. I believe his father owned the land once and he is buried not far from this place. I sent him on to the next world and saw the tunnel of light open for him and two men come to take his hand to take him up. He turned back and looked at me and Mr. Senate. It was so beautiful and I am glad I could help. I think Mr. Bill should not be invited back as he did little but scoff and make with the odd faces.

Mr. Senate is an old soul. I looked at him and saw an aged Monk. He was a teacher and spiritual man in his past lives. I am ready anytime to go and help spirits trapped on this earth. Thank you Mr. Senate for asking me to come.

Madam Helen, psychic medium

ABOUT THE AUTHOR

Richard Senate was born in Los Angeles, California, in 1948. His father, grandfather and uncles worked for MGM Studios in Culver City. His family moved to Thousand Oaks, California, when he was three. He grew up near the old Jungleland Wild Animal Park, where many films were made, including such forgettable TV shows as *Ramar of the Jungle* and *Sheena, Queen of the Jungle*. Richard's father, Leonard Senate, was once one of the three top banner men in the nation and was in demand as a circus decorator. Richard even helped his father paint circus wagons used in the movie, *The Big Circus* and the banner line for Disney Studio's *Toby Tyler.*

Richard attended Thousand Oaks High School, Ventura High School, Ventura Community College, Long Beach State and University of California at Santa Barbara. He holds a BA degree in History. He grew up hearing stories of ghosts in Hollywood, and strange happenings linked to the major studios. He didn't really become interested in the subject of ghosts until 1978, when he saw a phantom monk at one of the old Spanish Missions. This was such a profound event, that it caused him to take up psychic research in an attempt to find an answer to this mystery.

Mr. Senate lectures at California State University at Northridge, Pierce College and (in the past) Ventura College. He resides in Ventura, California. He writes a column for the *Ojai and Ventura Voice* Newspaper. He has appeared on numerous TV and Radio programs over the years including *Sightings*, *The Travel Channel* Specials and the *Merv Griffin Show* where he has spoken as an expert on the subject of ghosts and the supernatural.

He is the author of nine published books. Many of his works deal with the subject of ghosts and the supernatural and local history. His five newest books are *Ghosts of Ventura, Ghosts of the Ojai, Ghosts of El Camino Real, Historic Adobes of Ventura County, and Hollywood's Ghosts.* He is currently published by Del Sol Publications. www.delsolpublications.com Also available: *Ghosts of the Haunted Coast* (Pathfinder Publishing) *The Haunted Southland, Erle Stanley Gardner's Ventura and The Ghost Stalker's Guide to Haunted California* (Charon press).

His web site on the internet was the very first on the subject of ghosts and recently won two awards. It is located at www.ghost-stalker.com

Photo Megan Senate

Richard Senate